Got Skulls

Tattoo Coloring Book

ISBN 13: 978-1-948187-31-2
ISBN 10: 1-948187-31-0

All images are on file with The Library of Congress

Published by

Cort's Royal Ink Tattoo Company

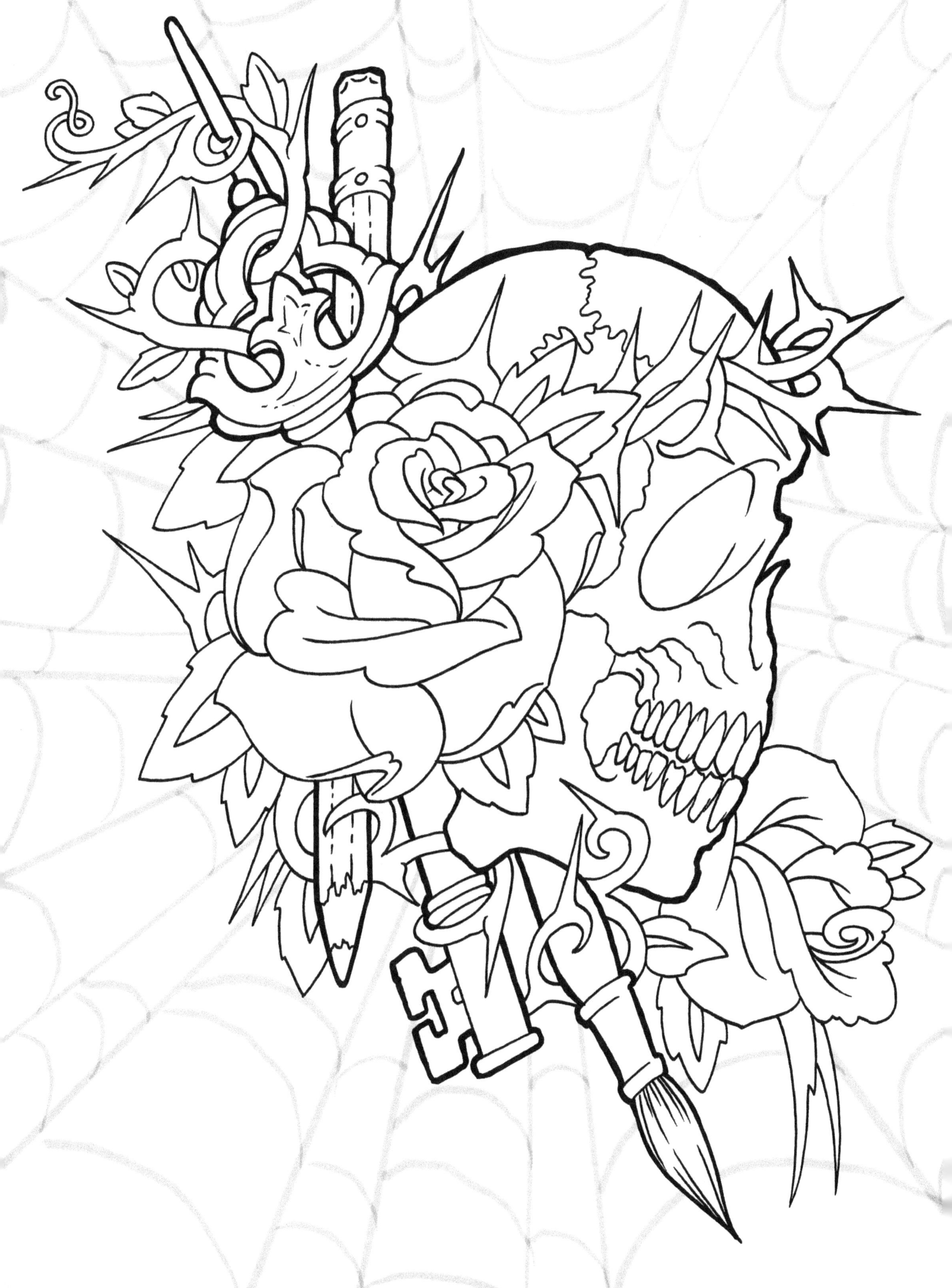

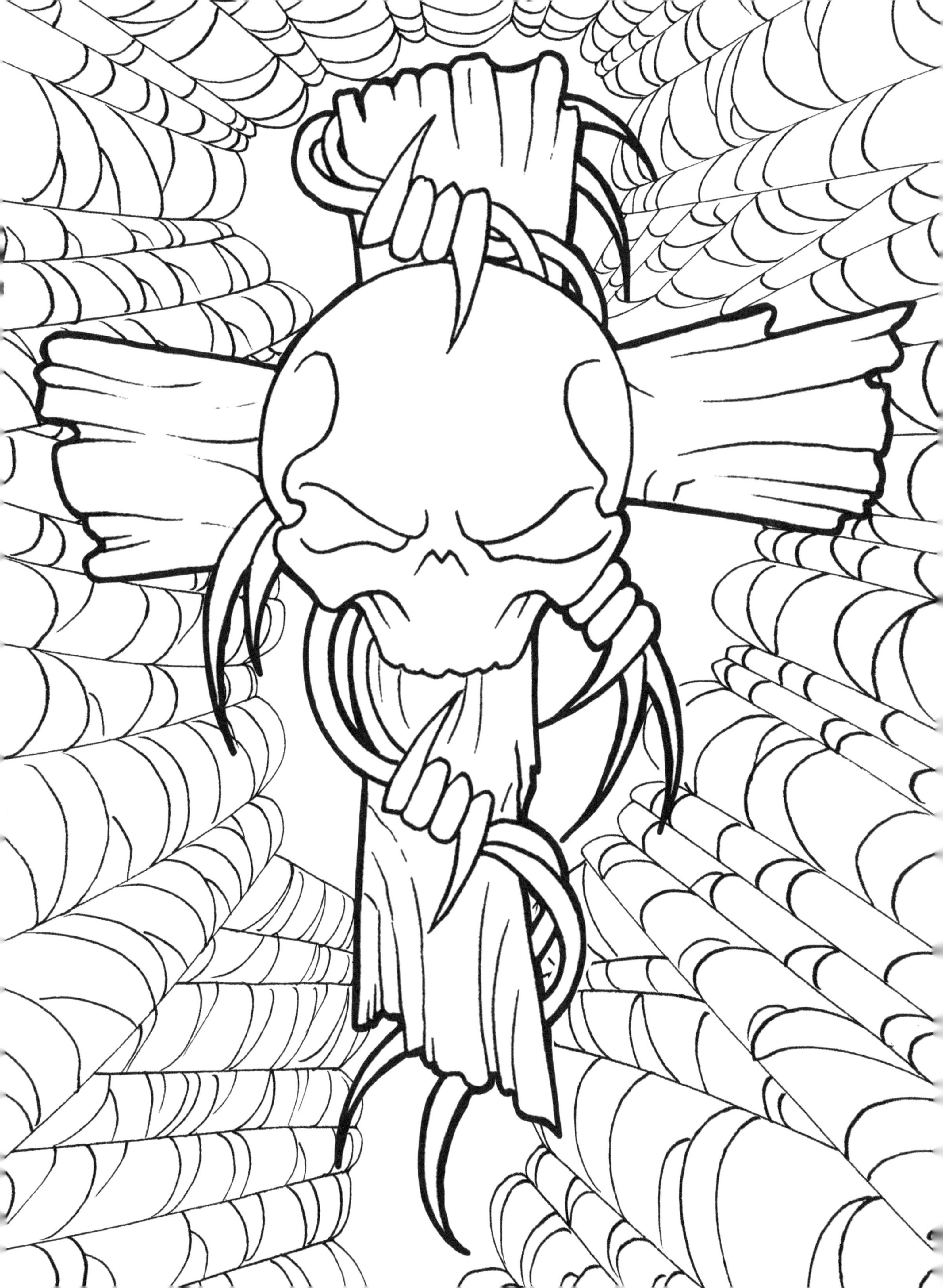

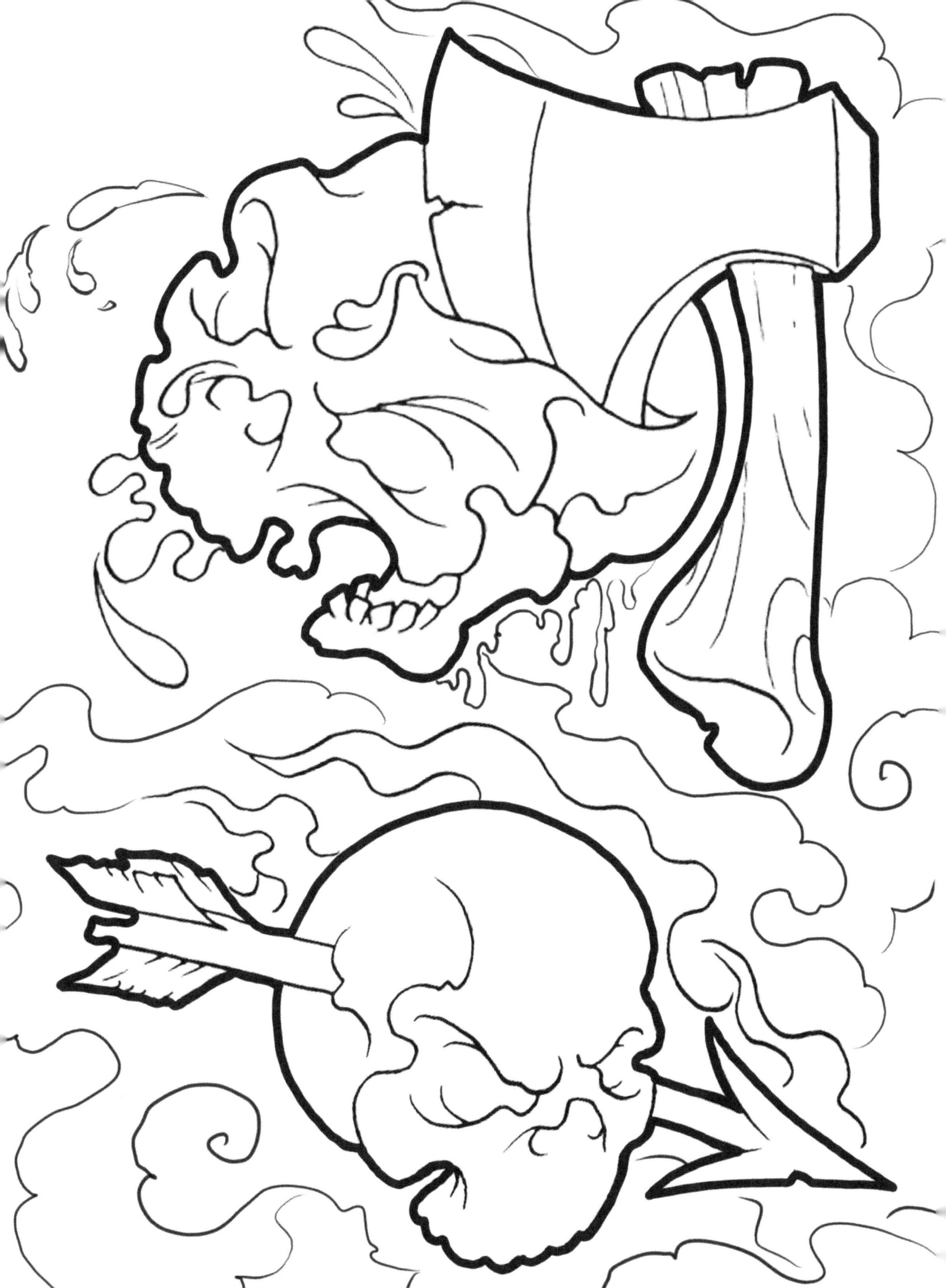

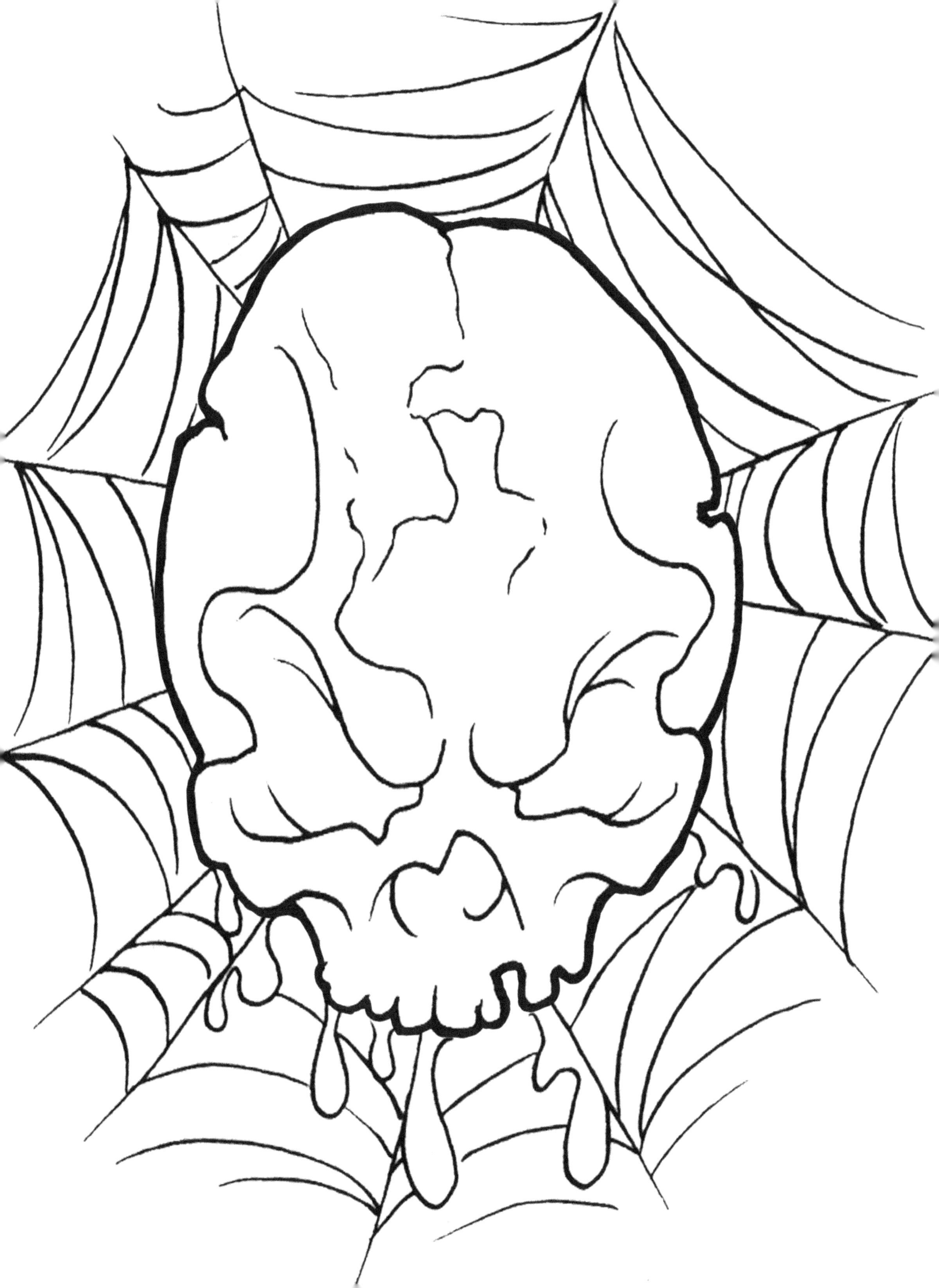

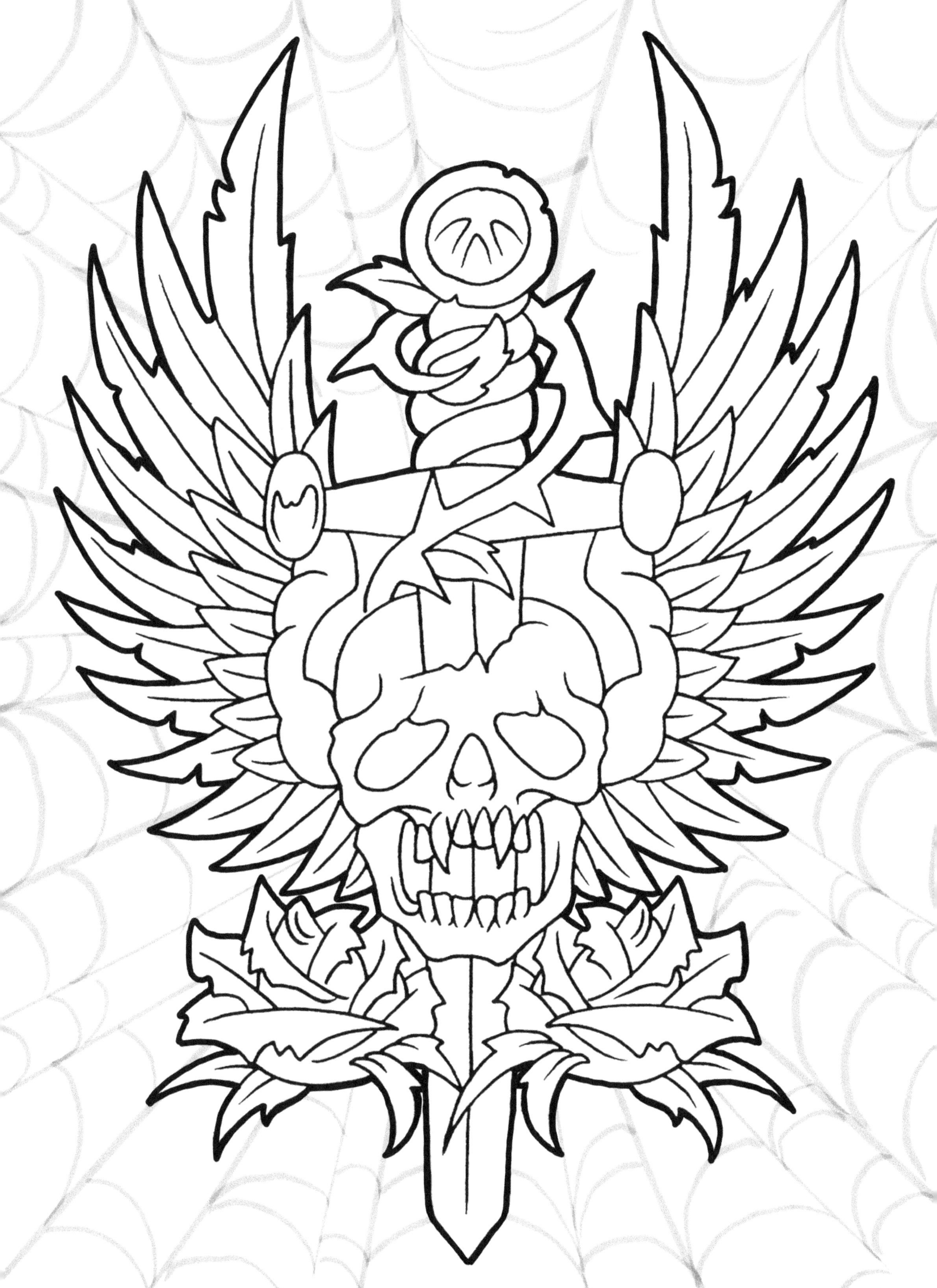

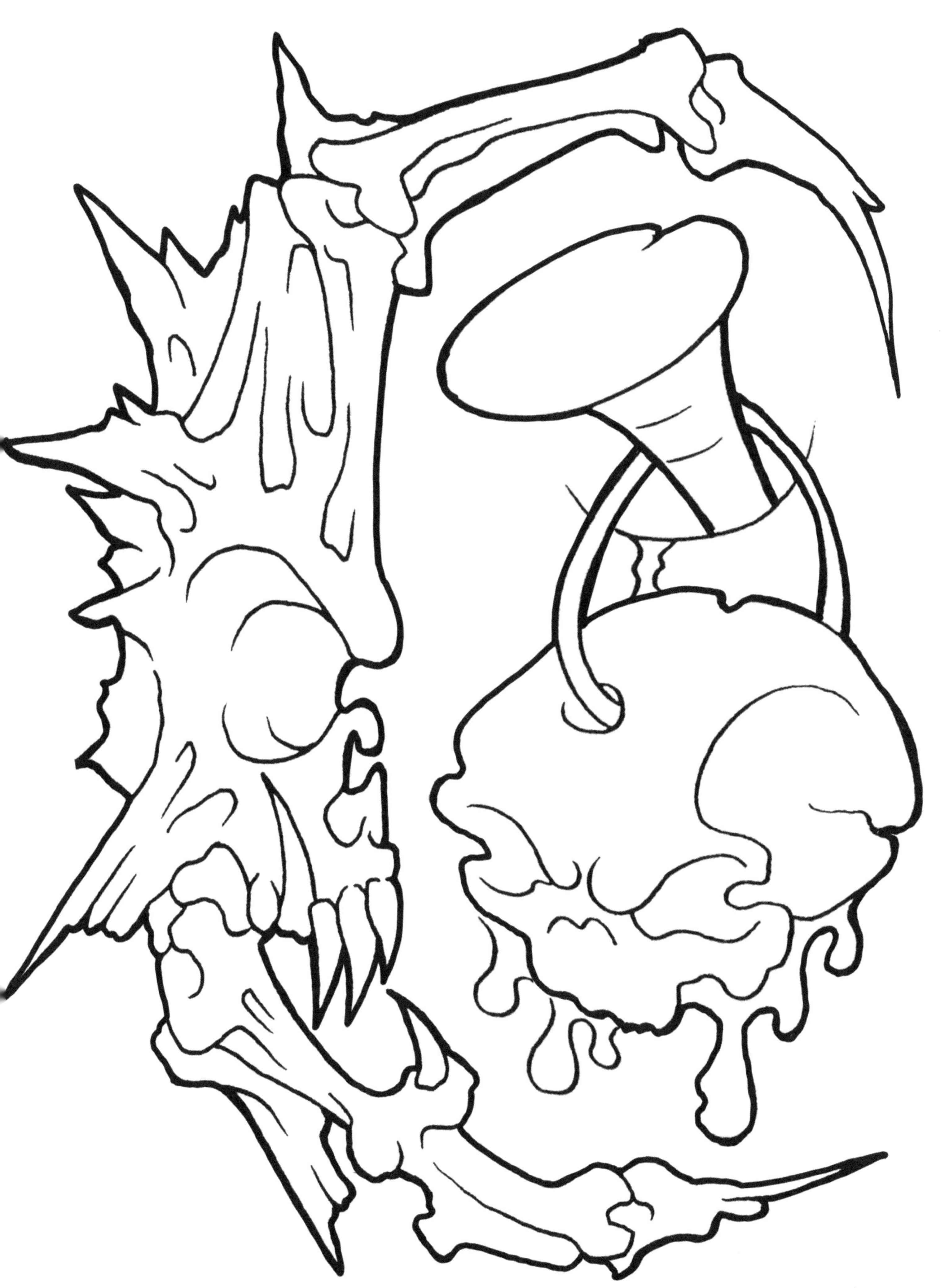

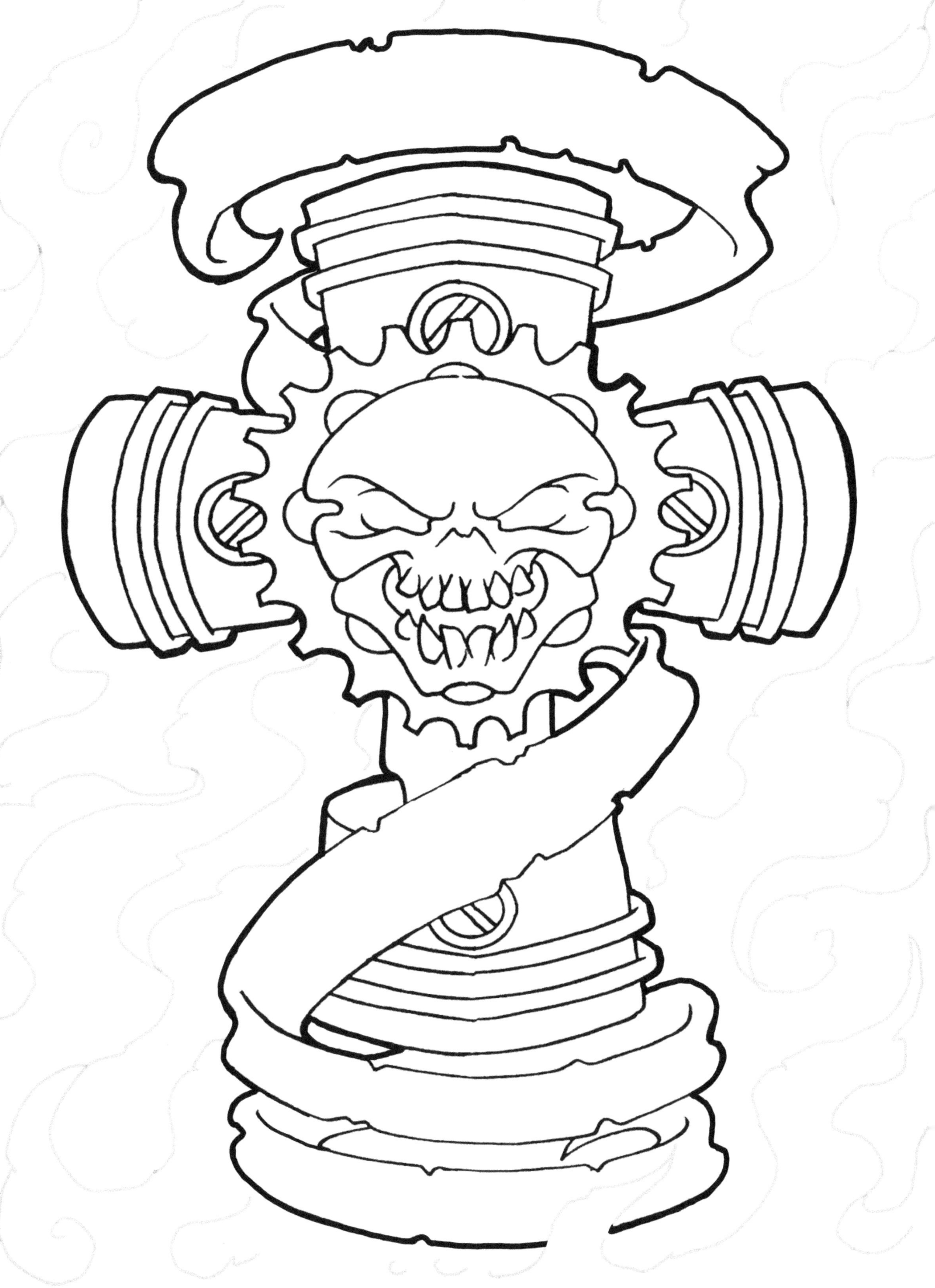

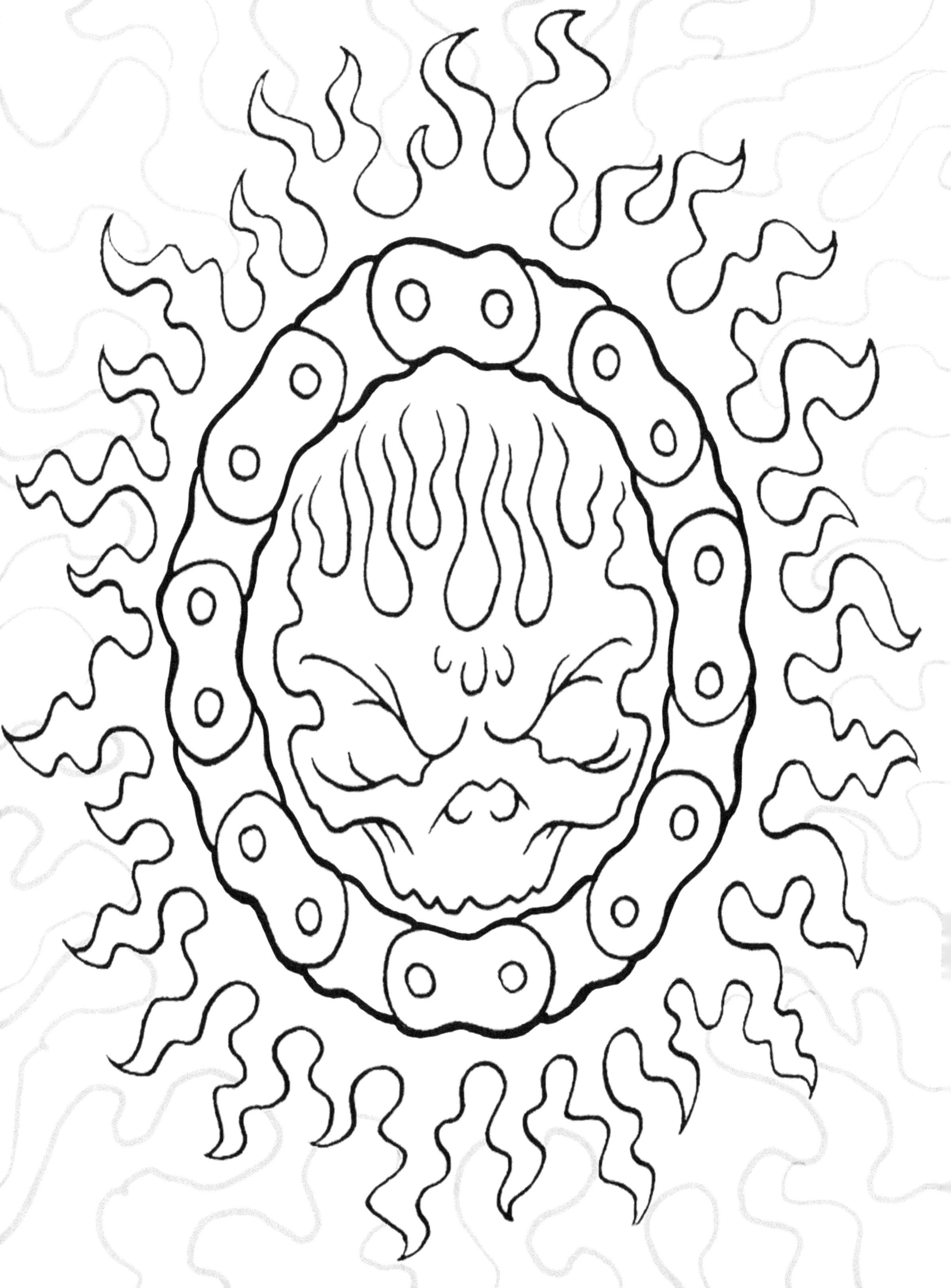

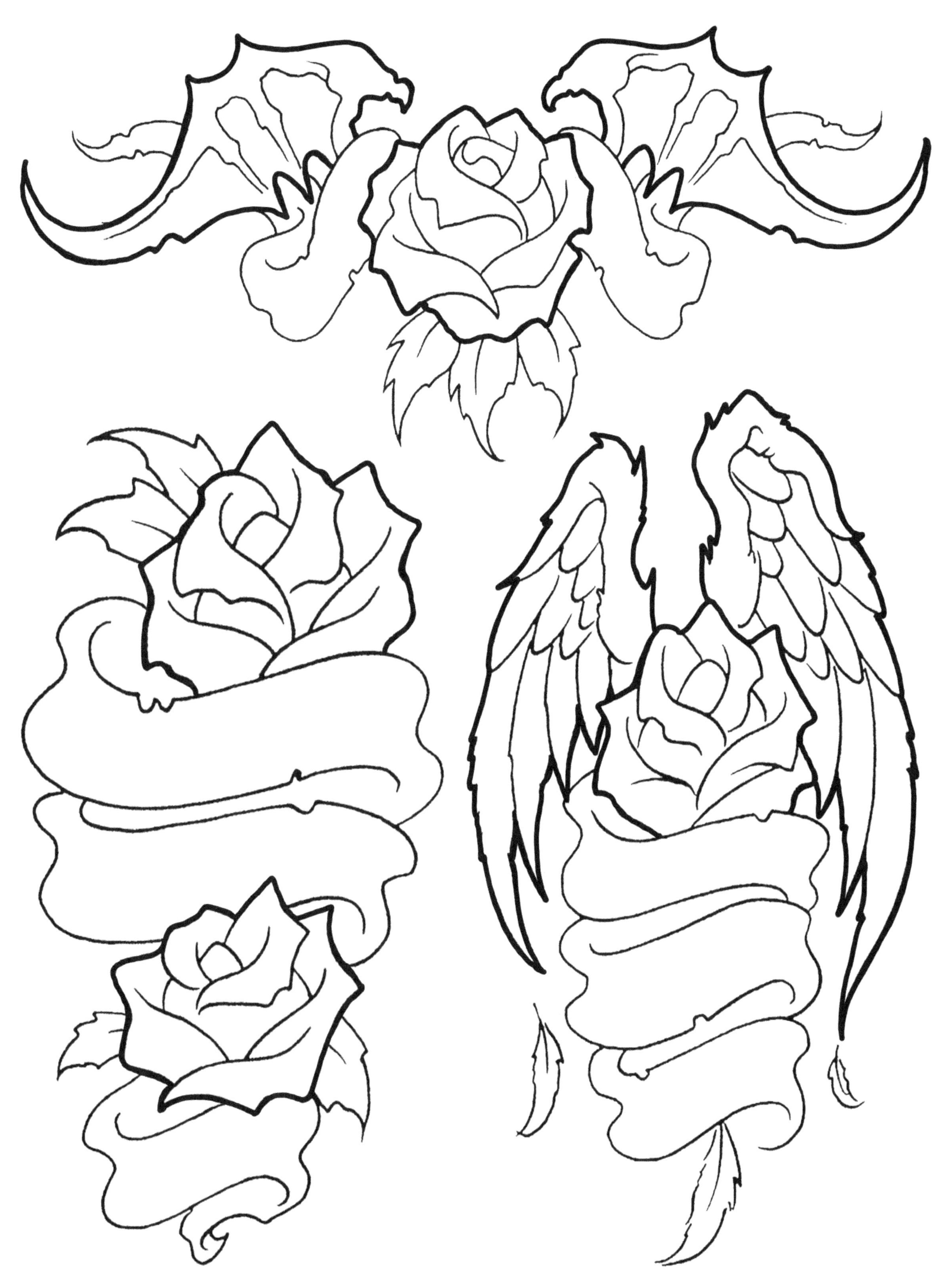

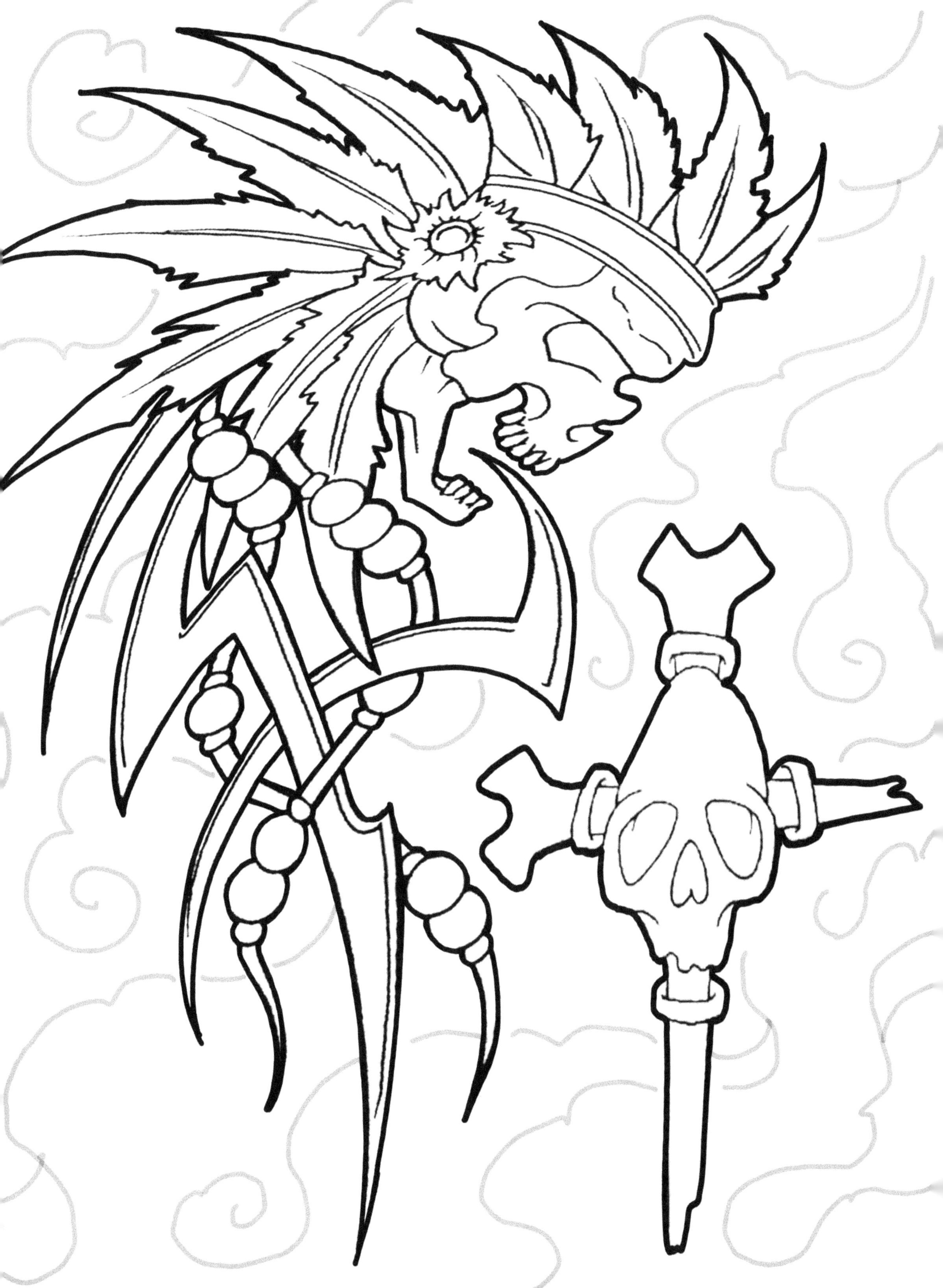

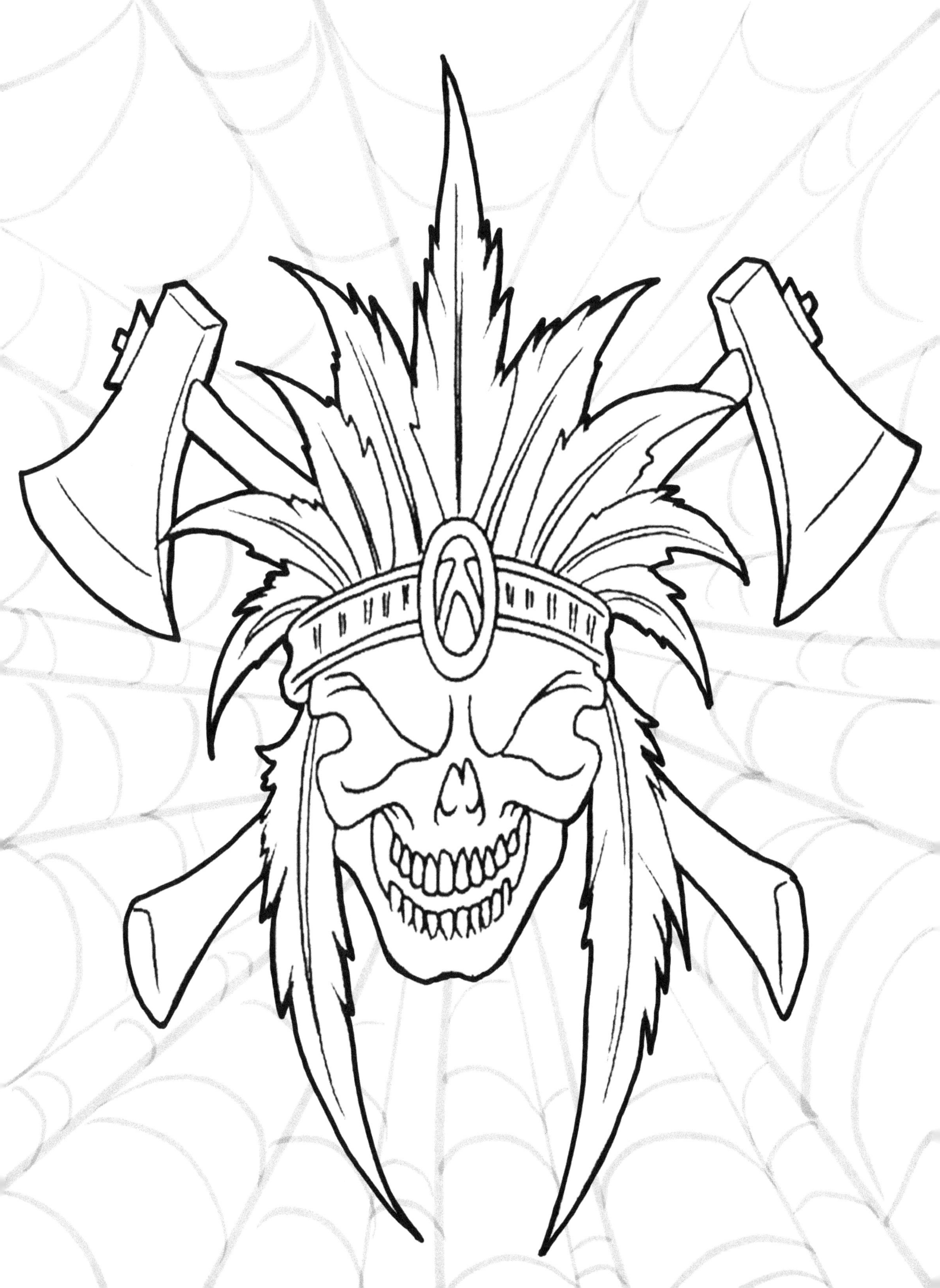

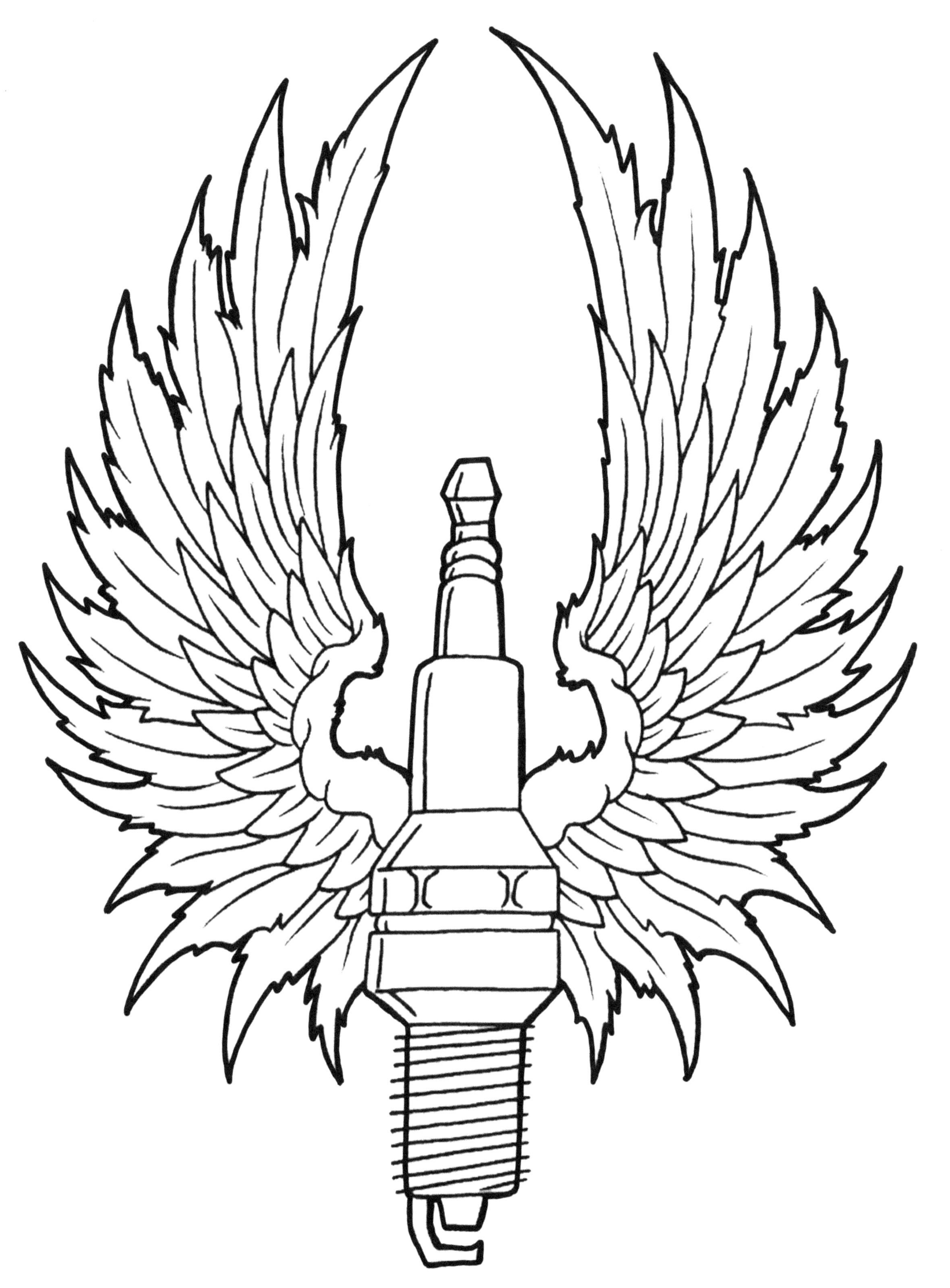

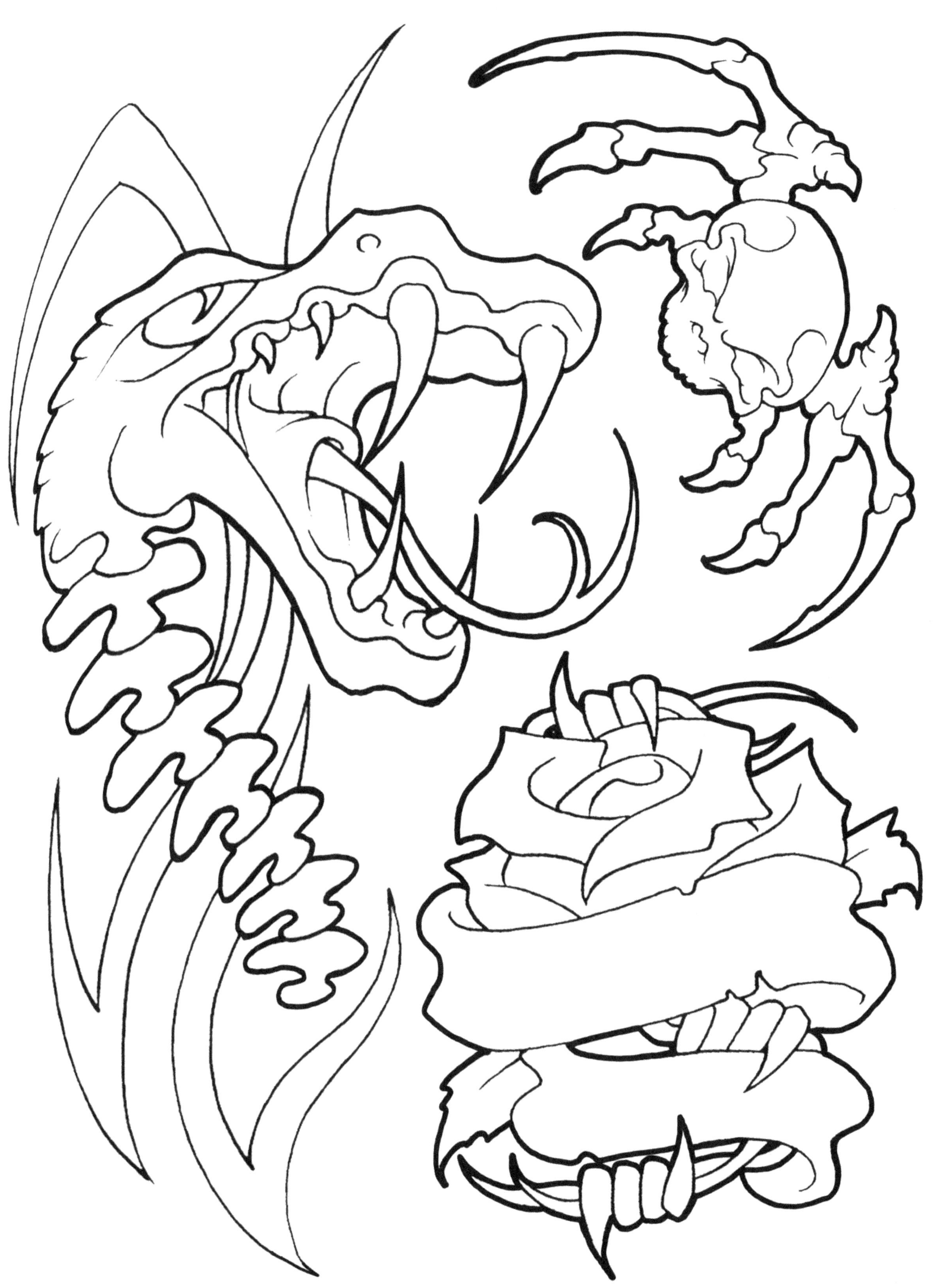

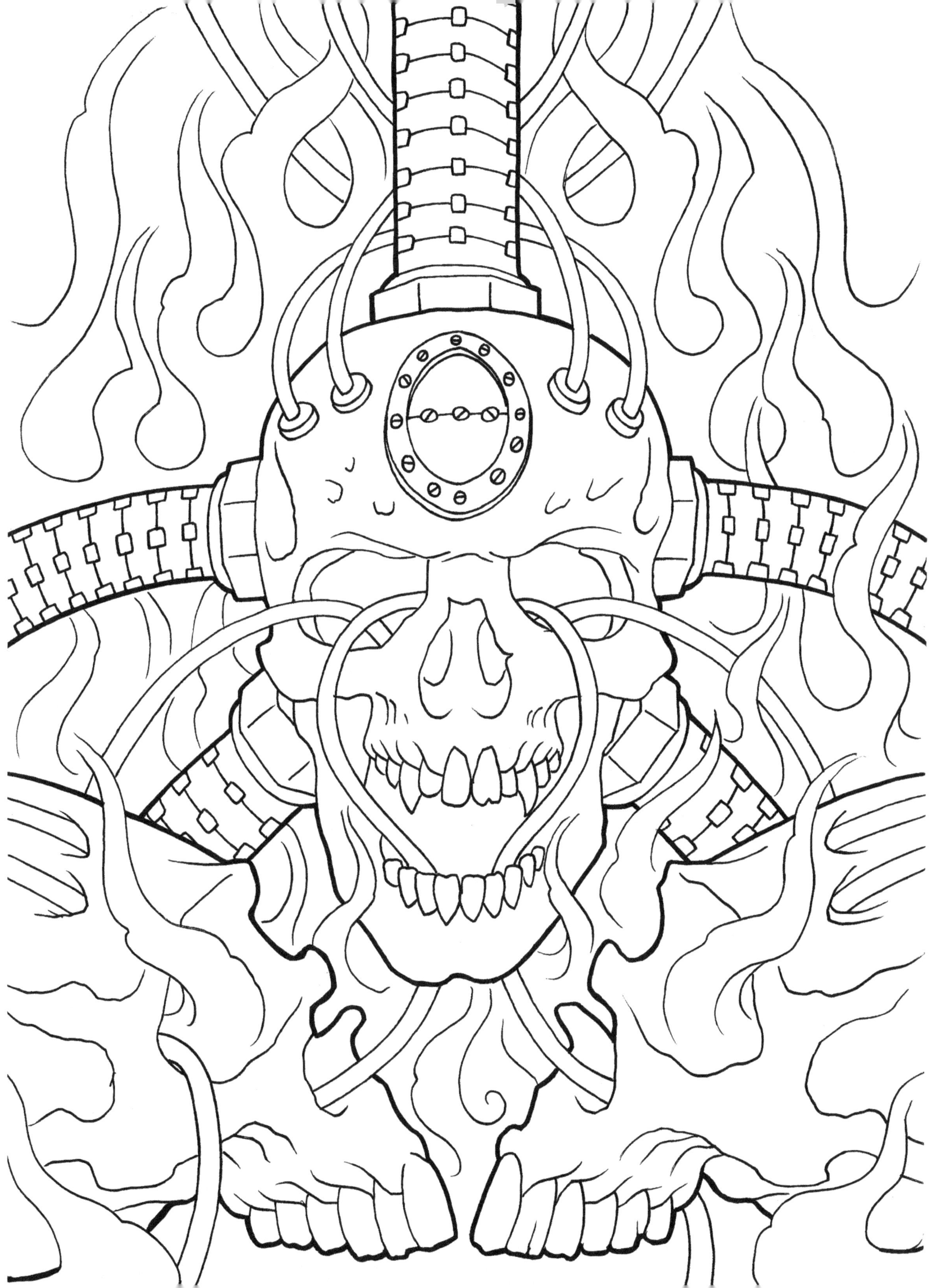

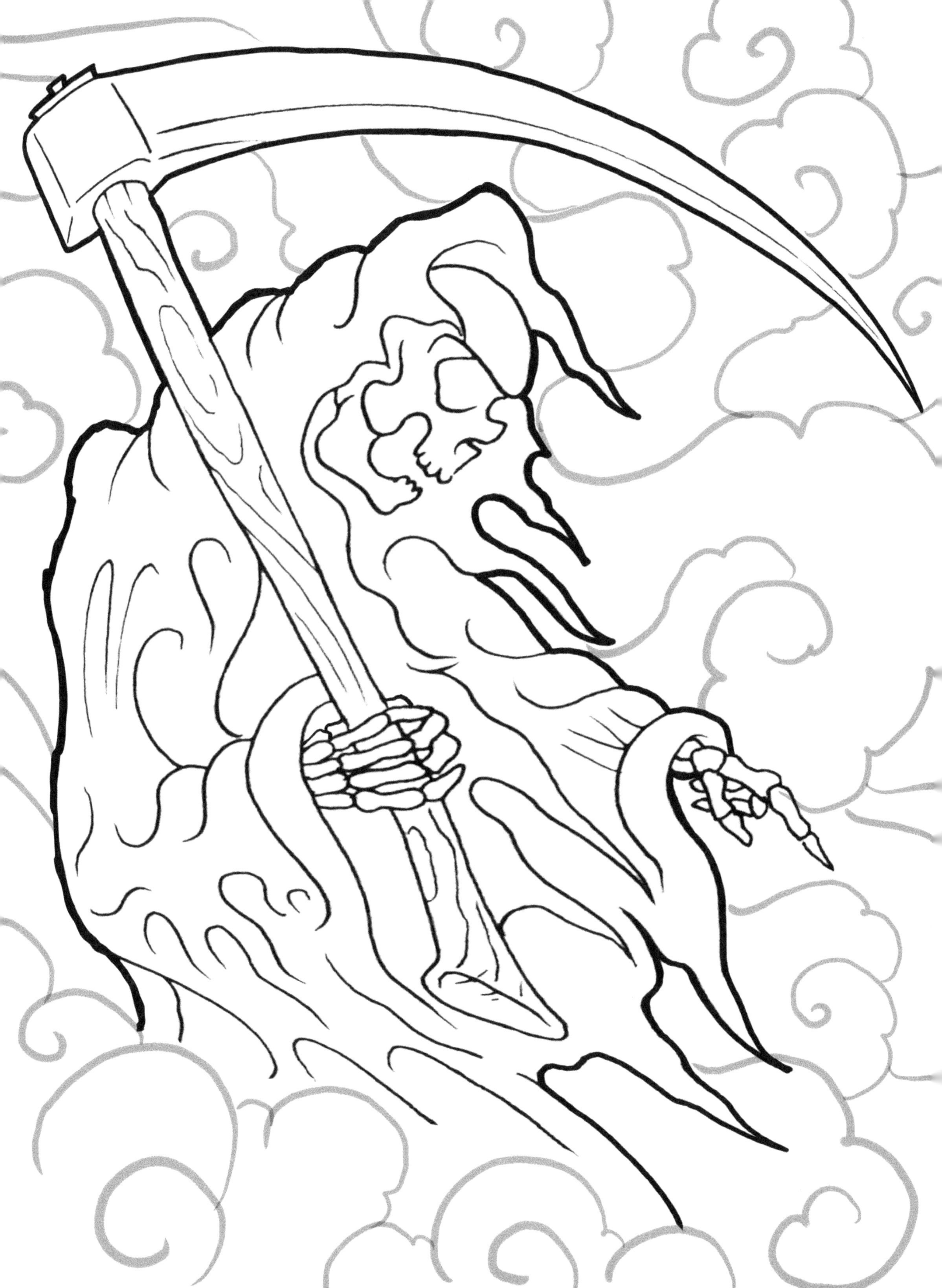

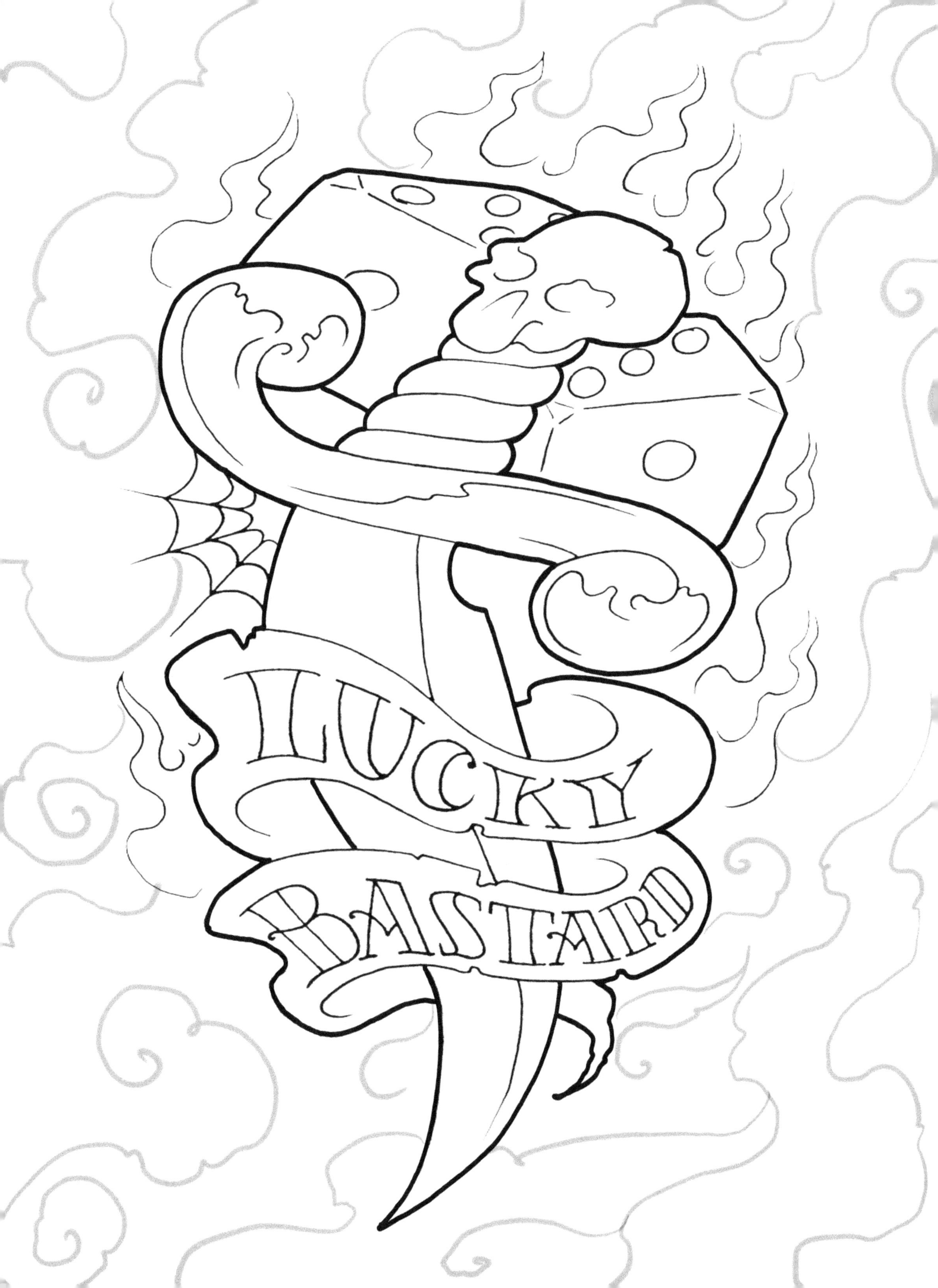
LUCKY
BASTARD

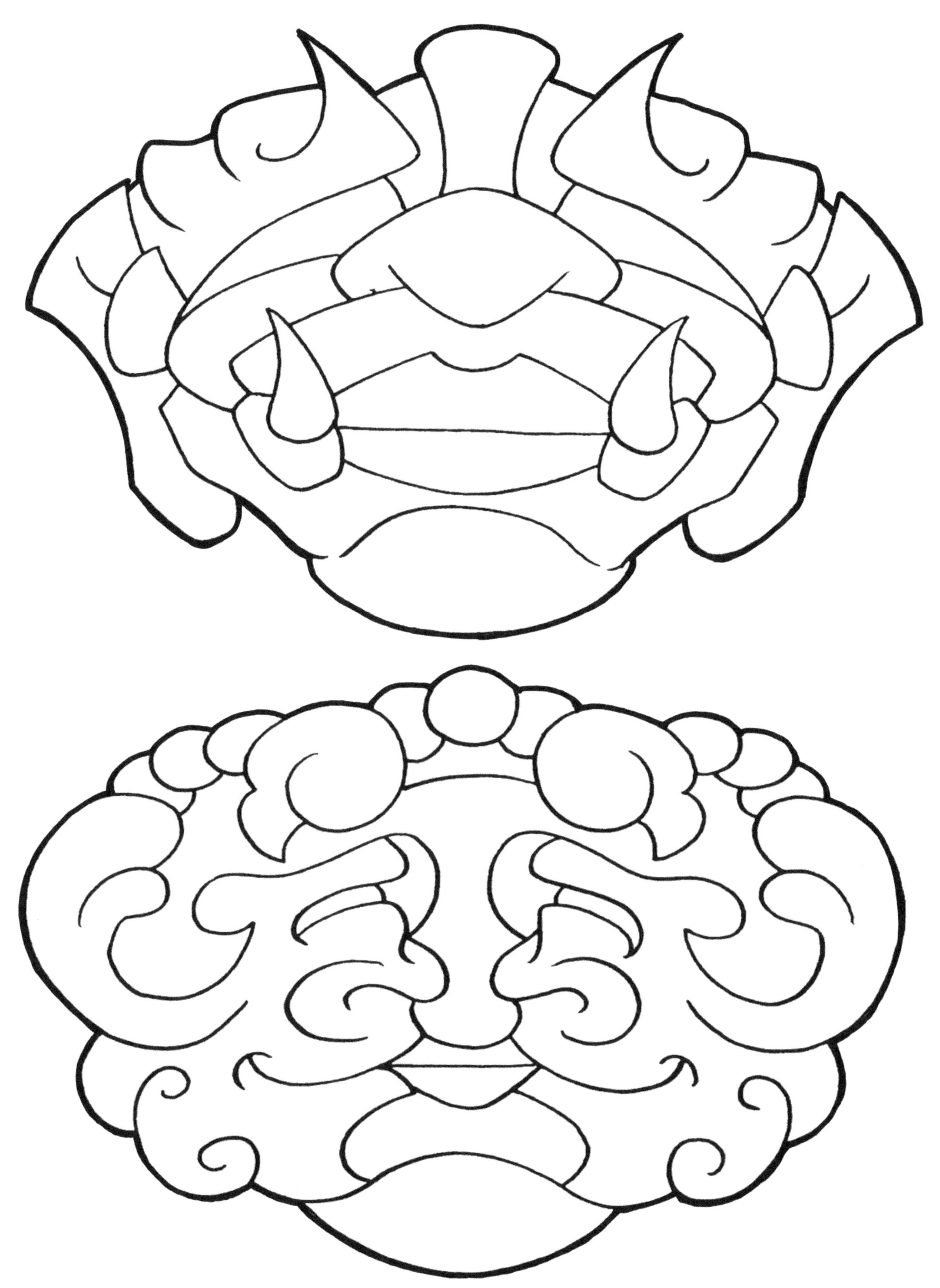

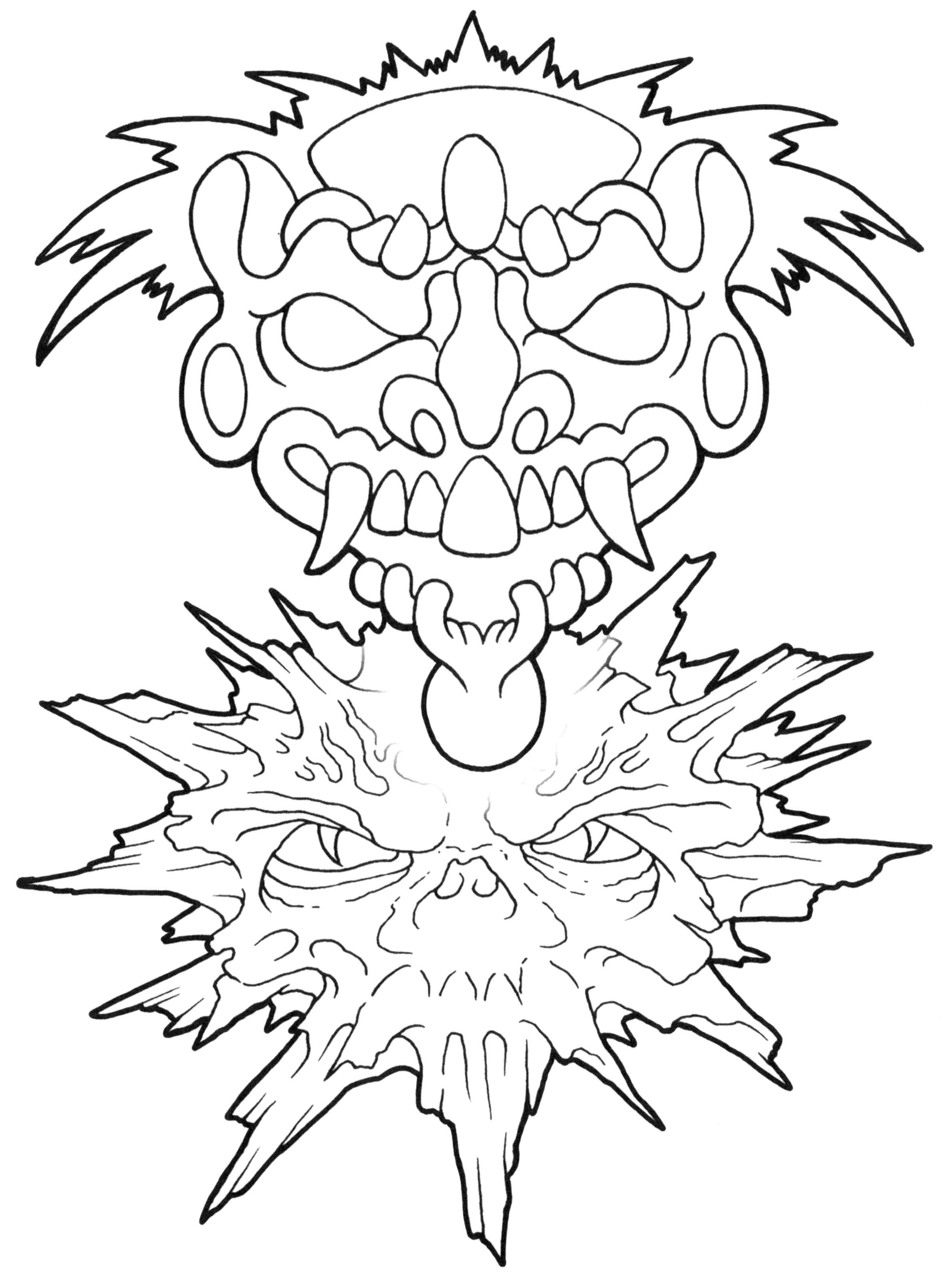

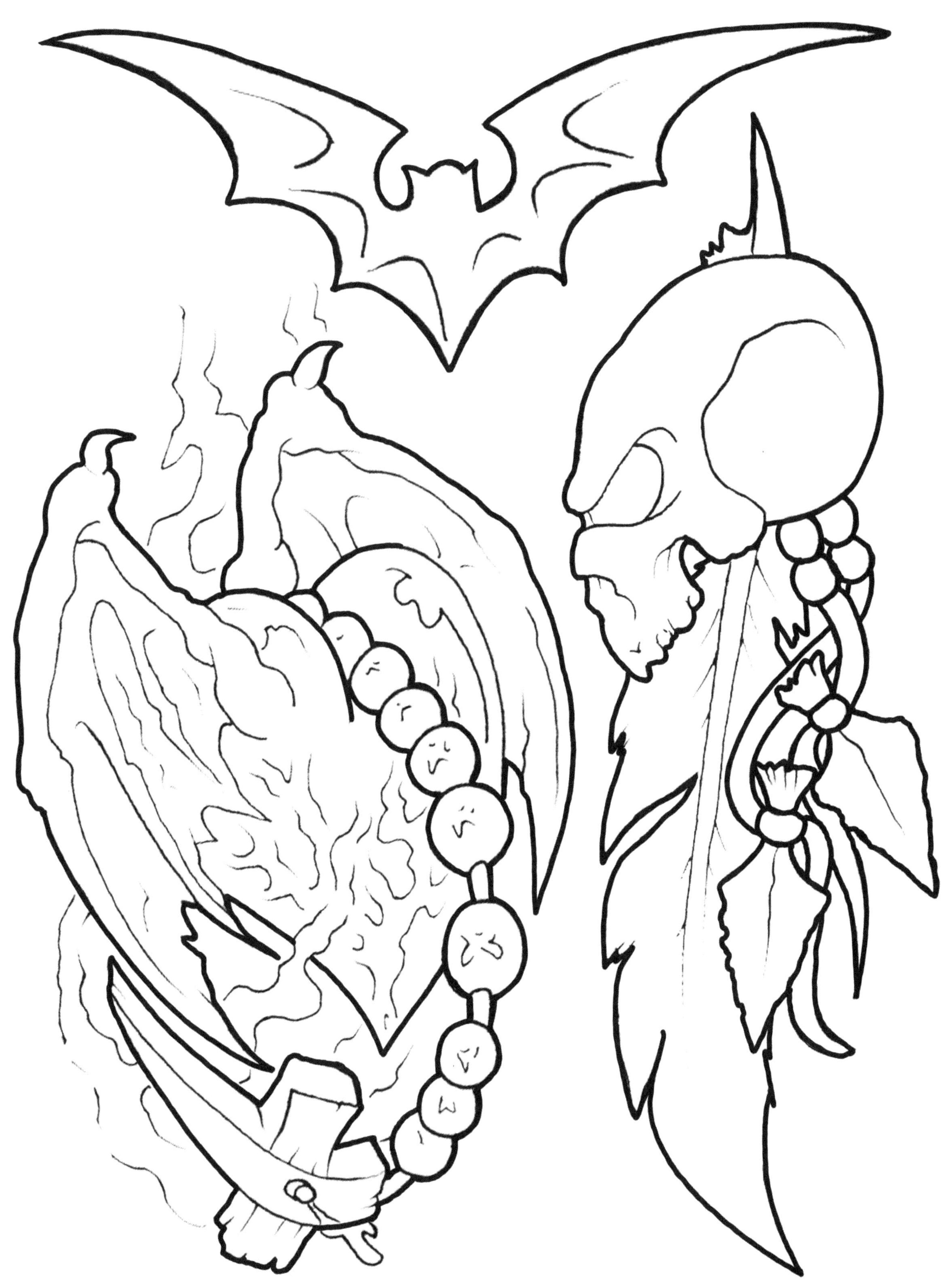

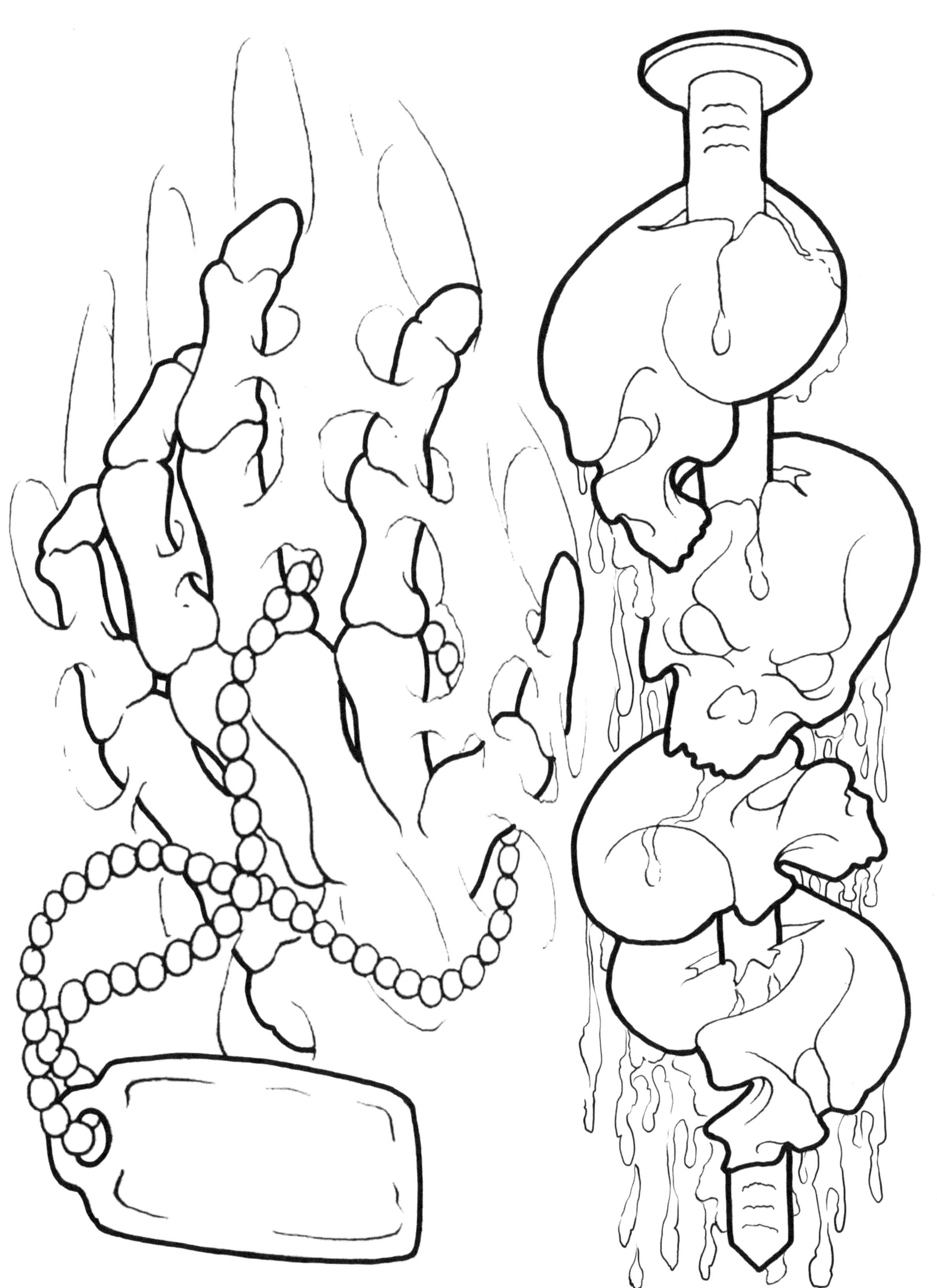

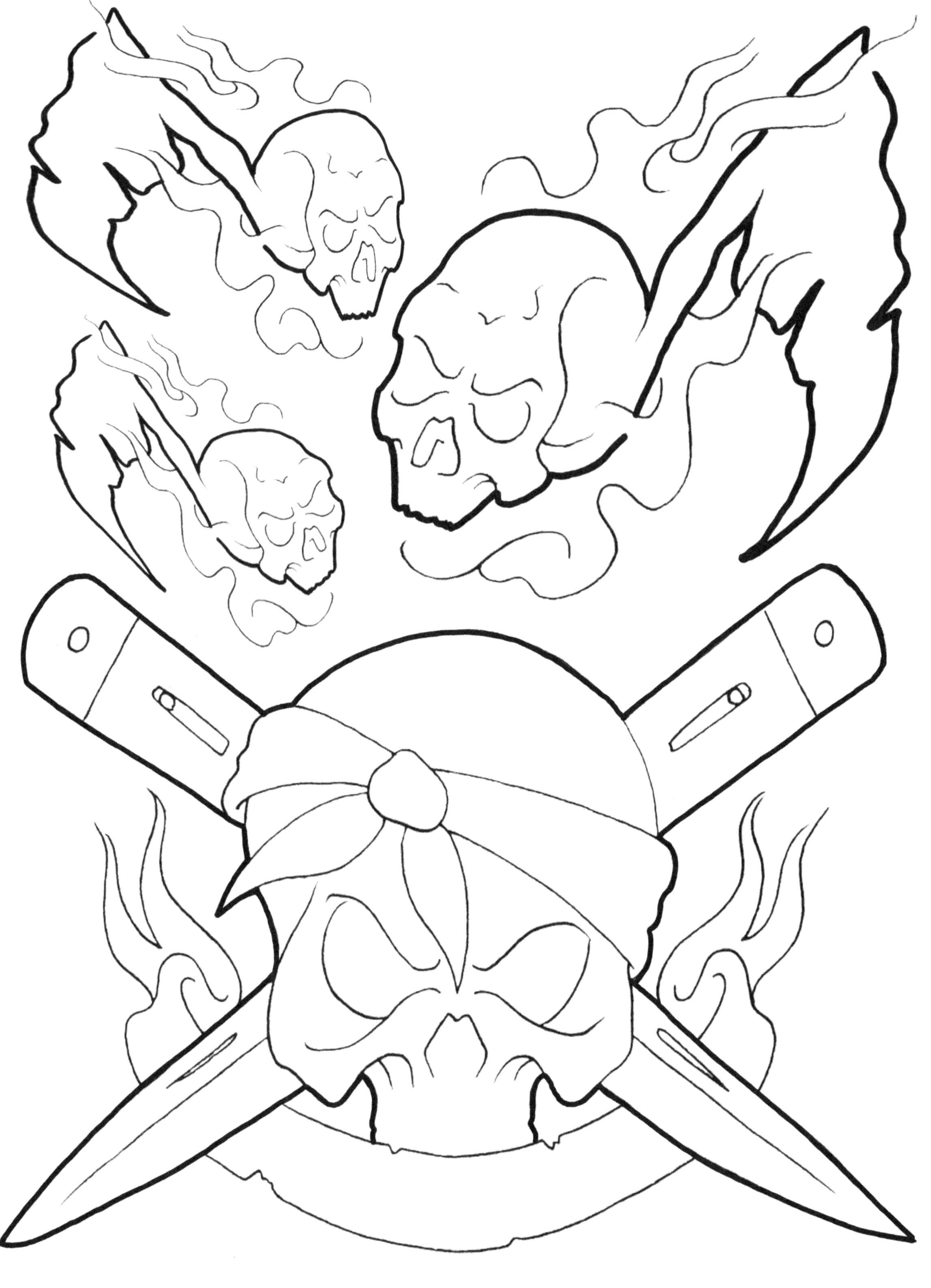

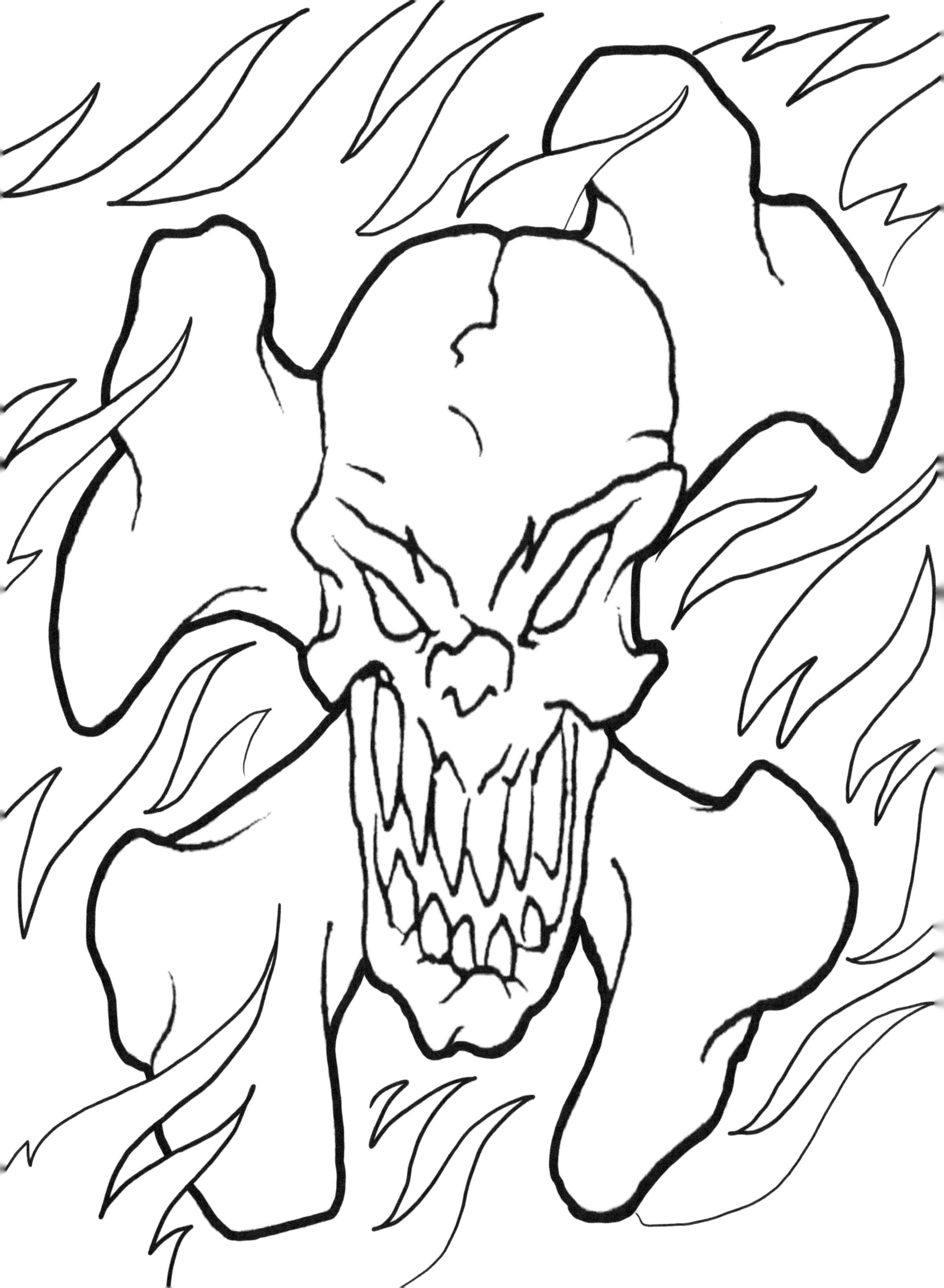

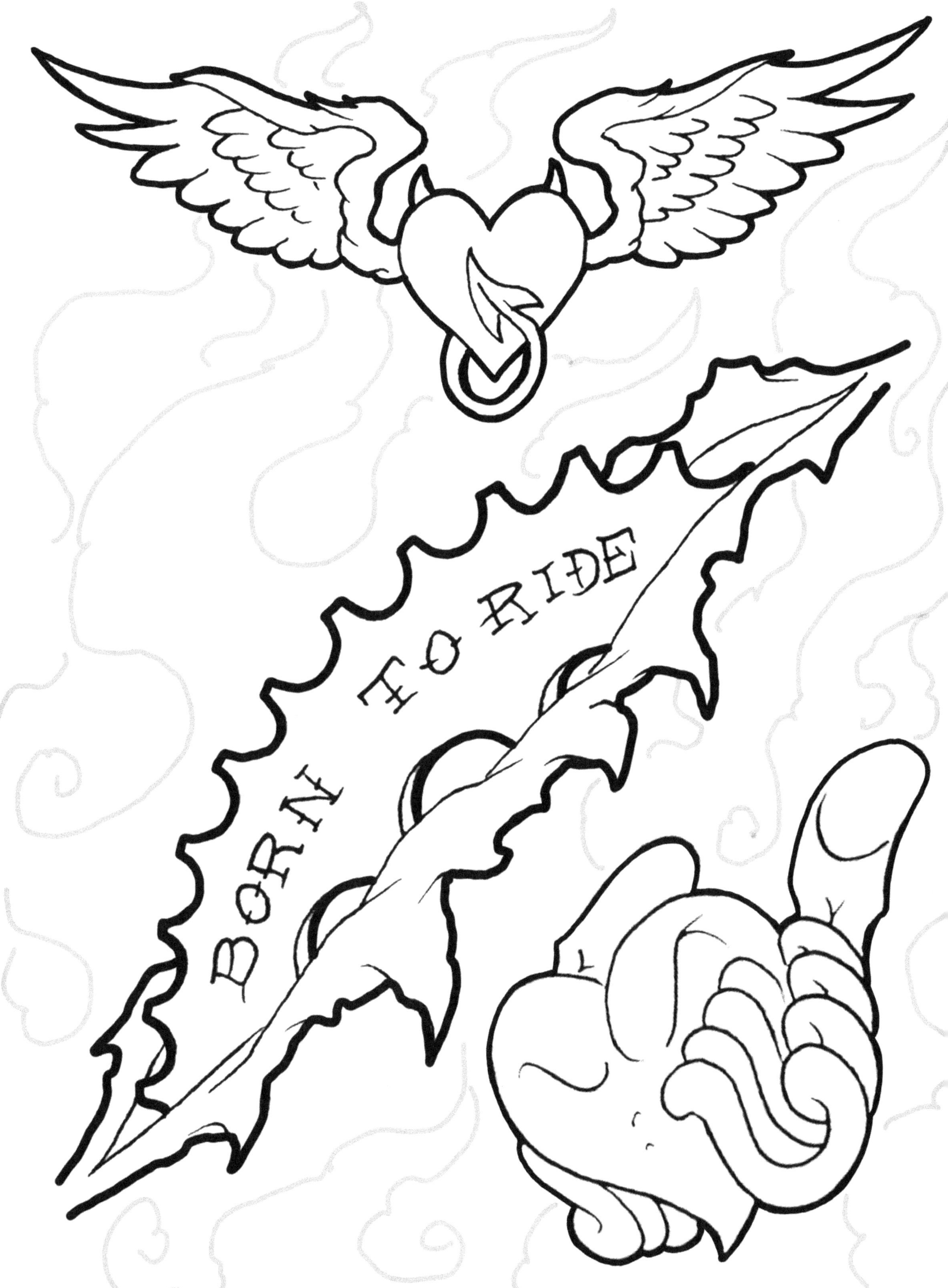
BORN TO RIDE

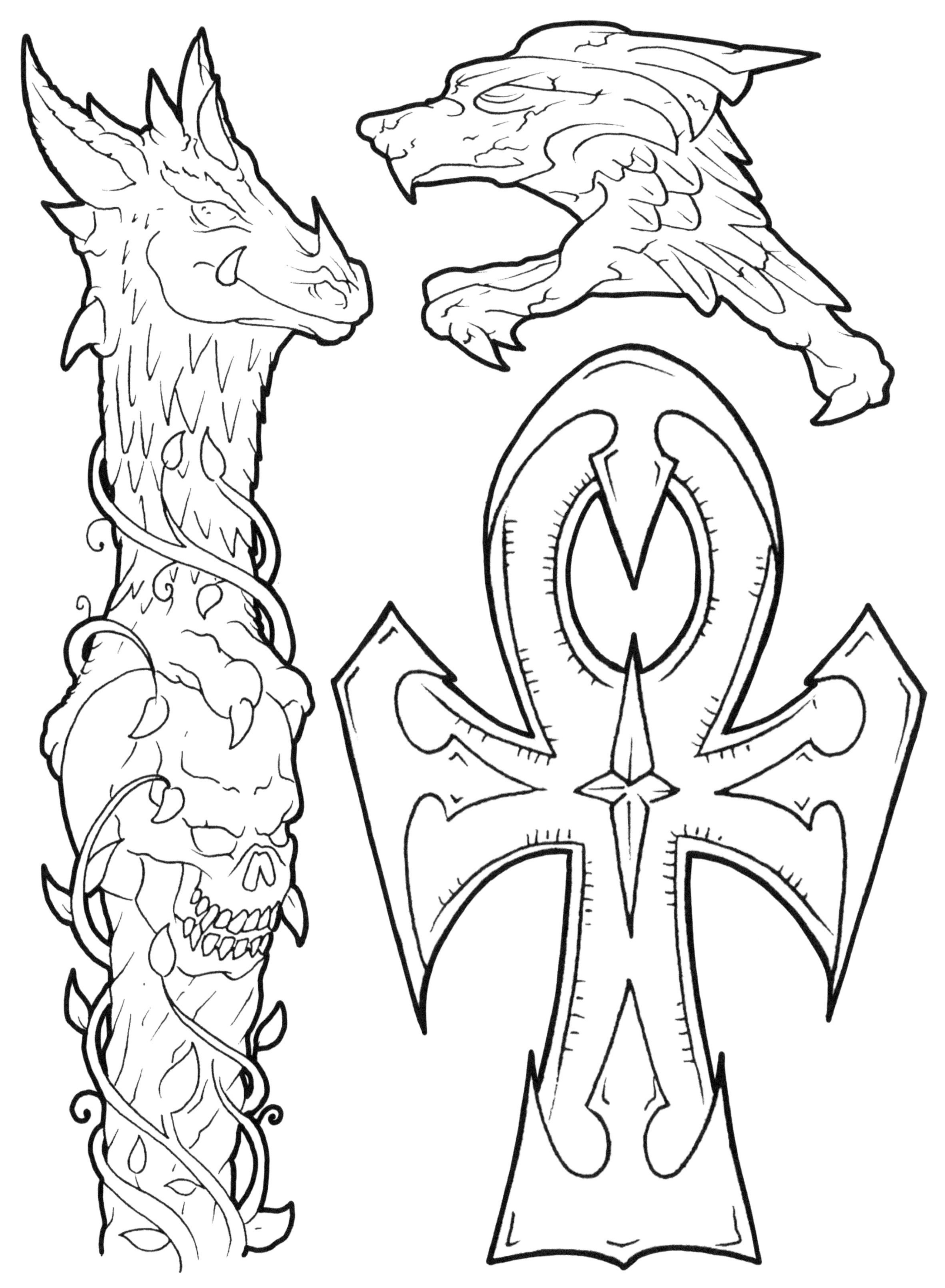

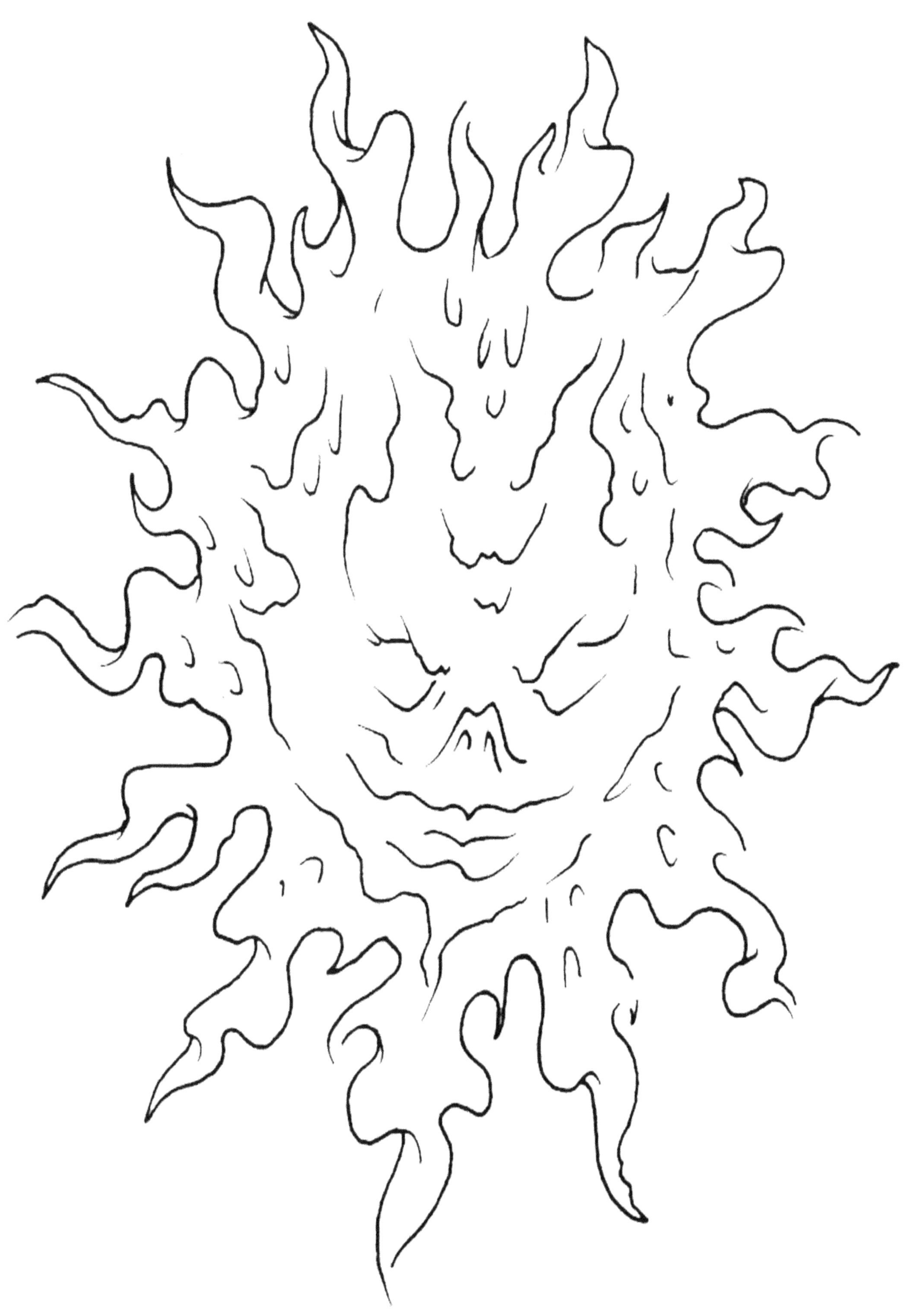

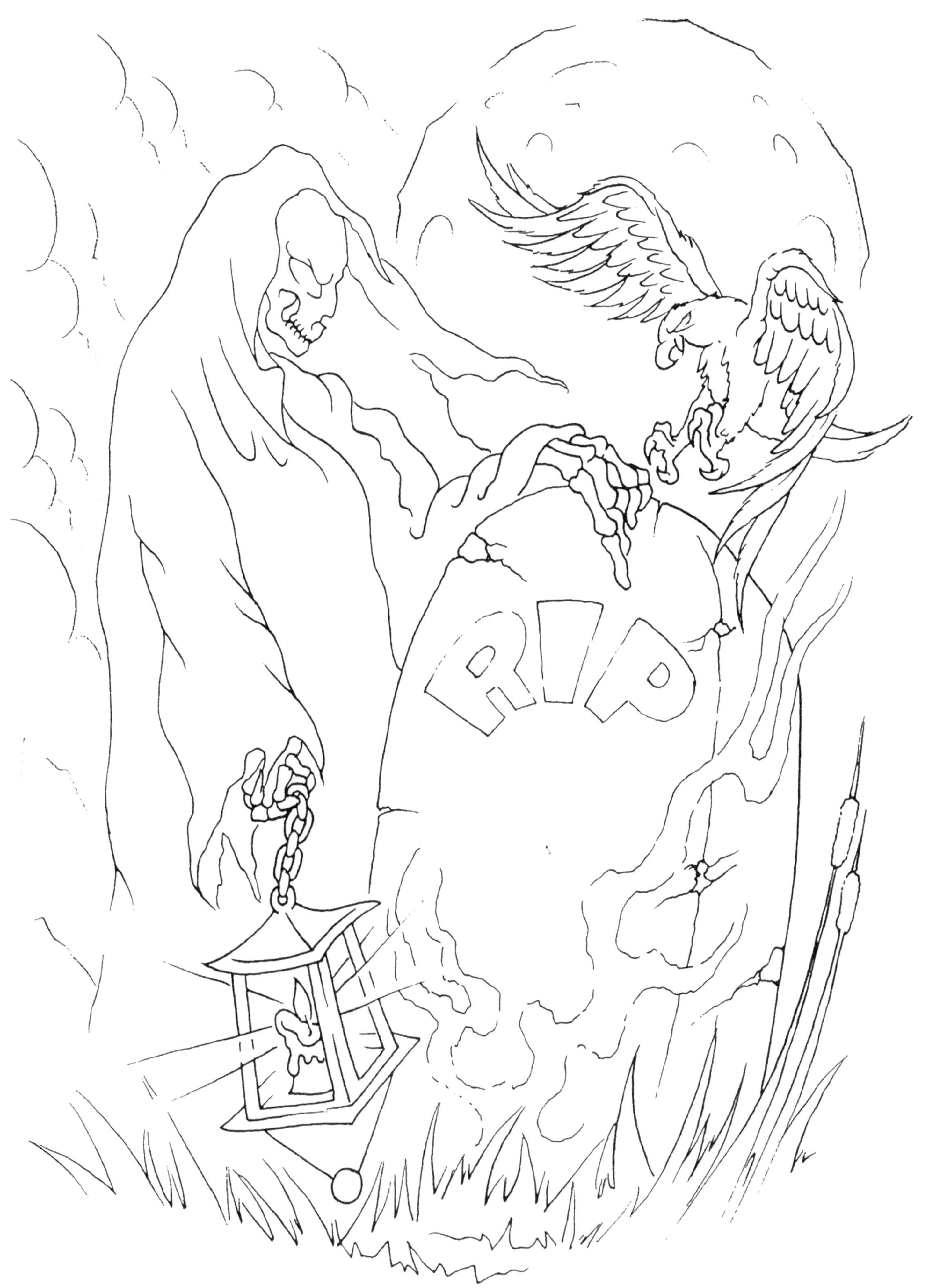
RIP

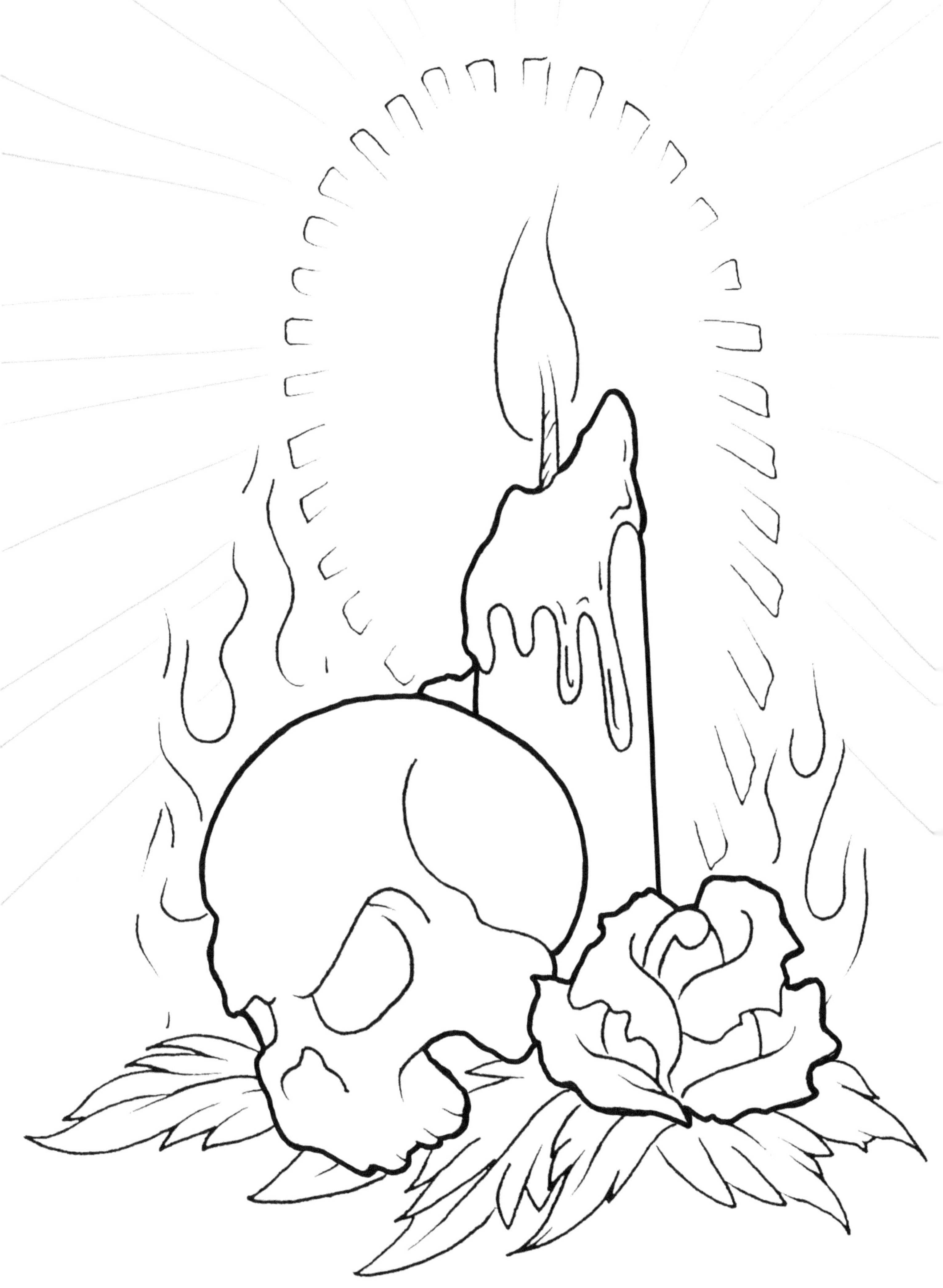

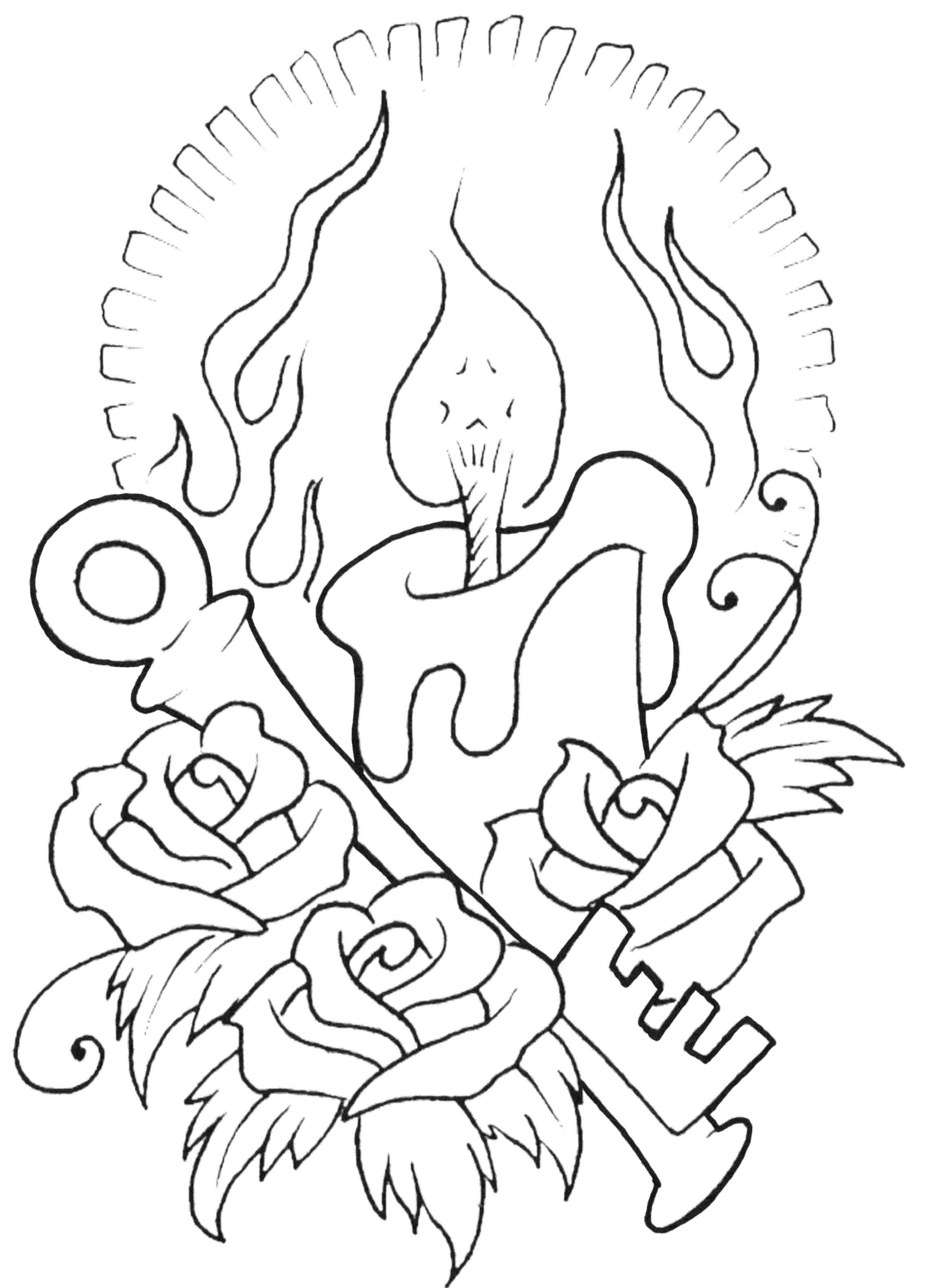

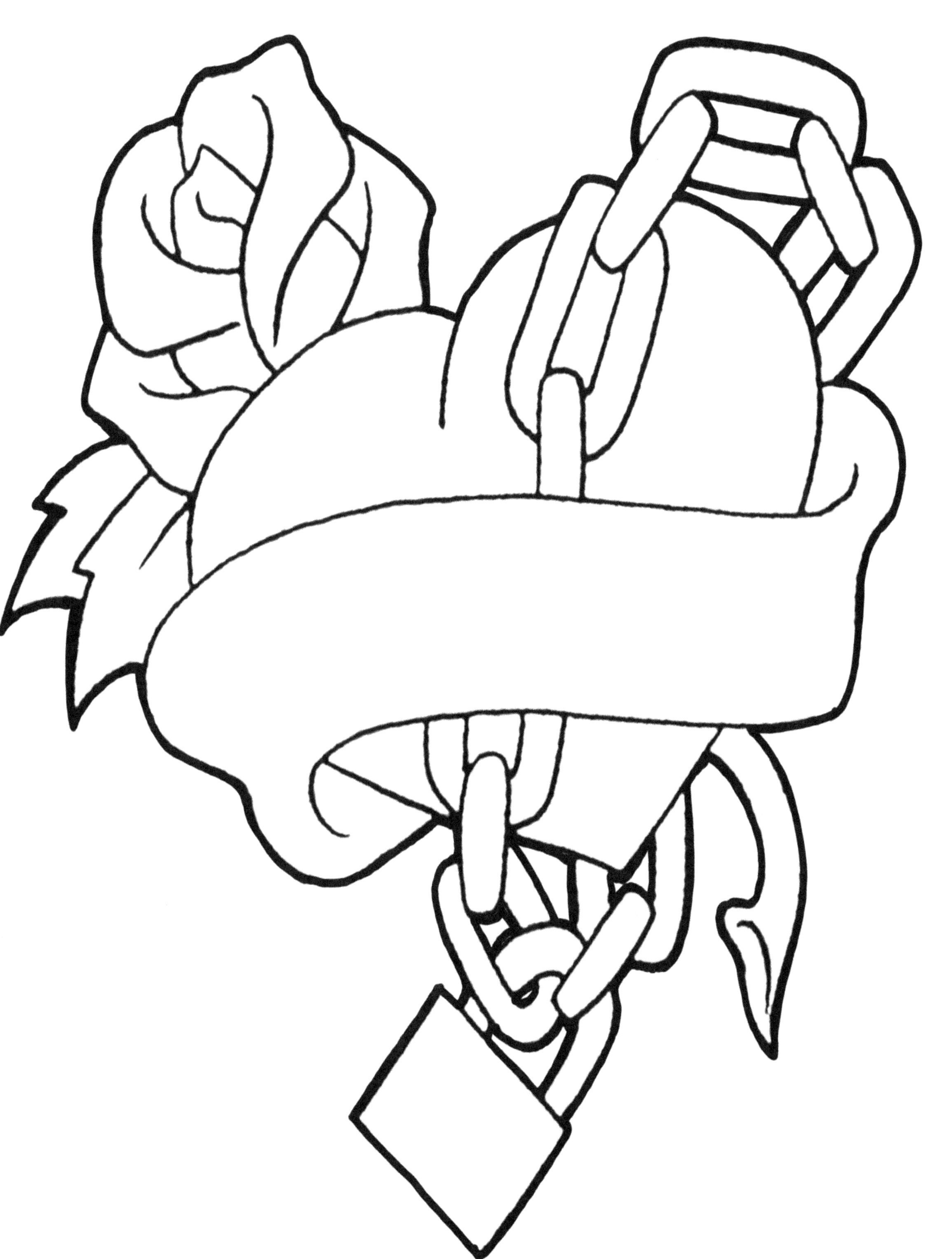

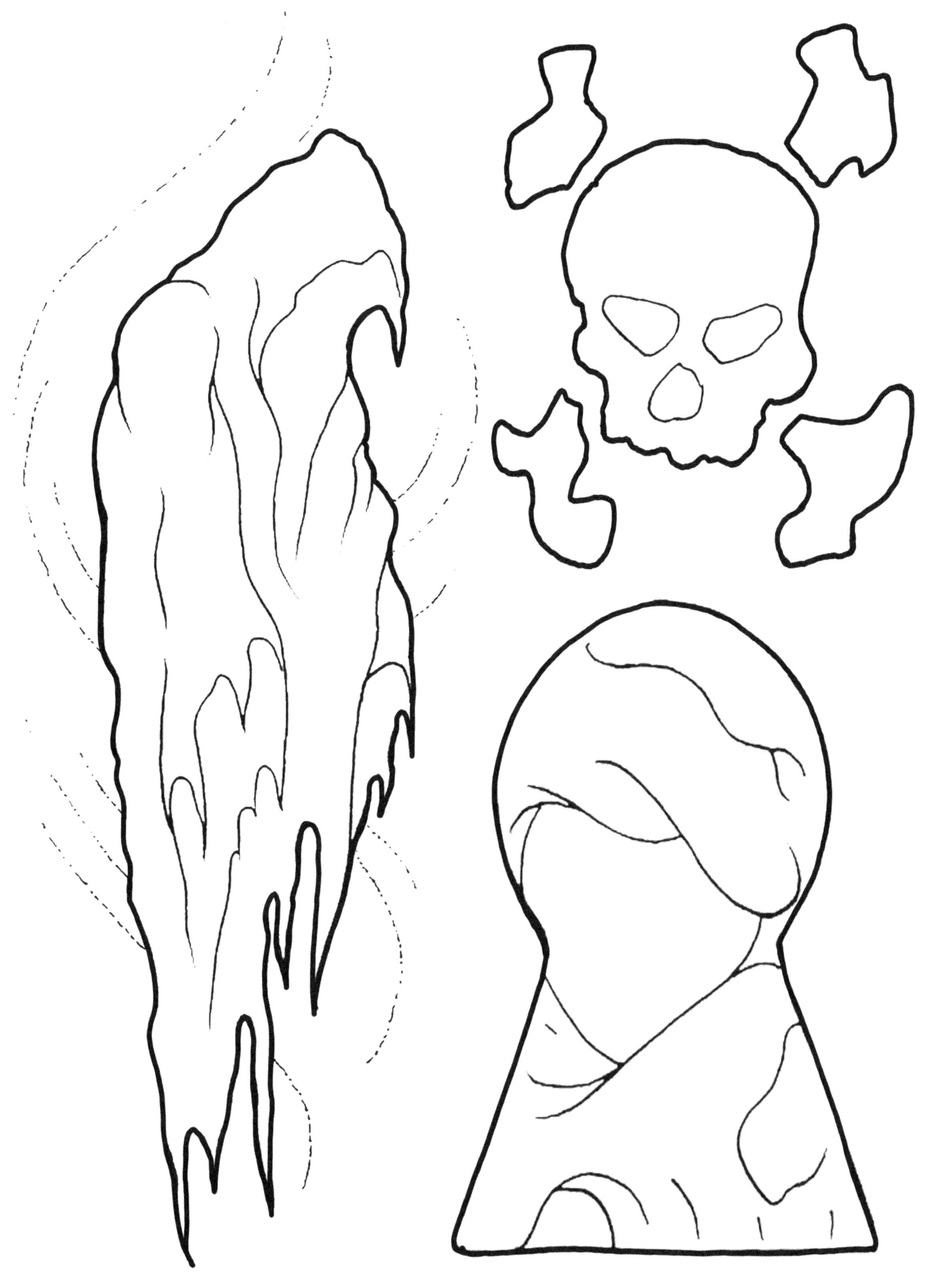

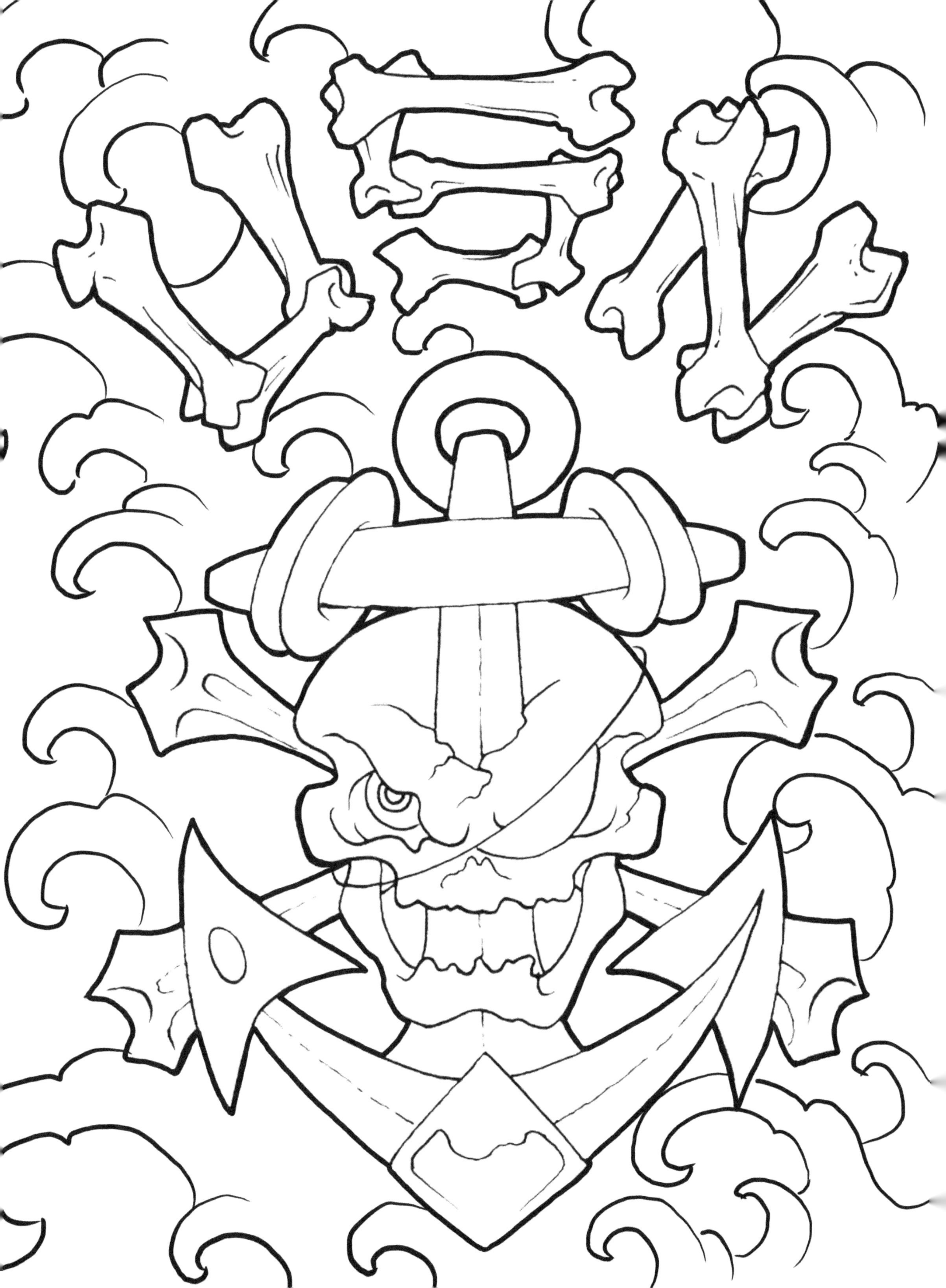

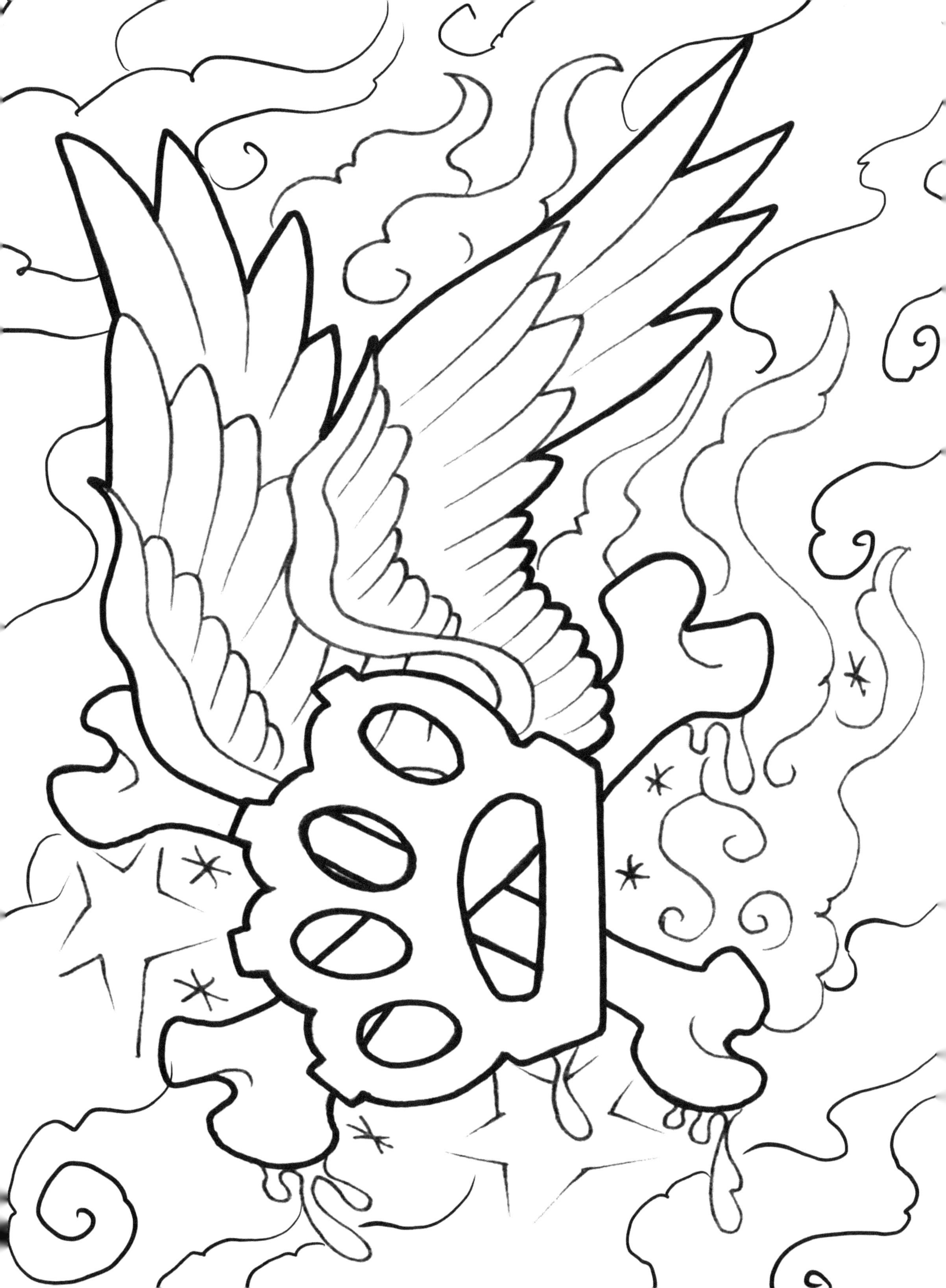

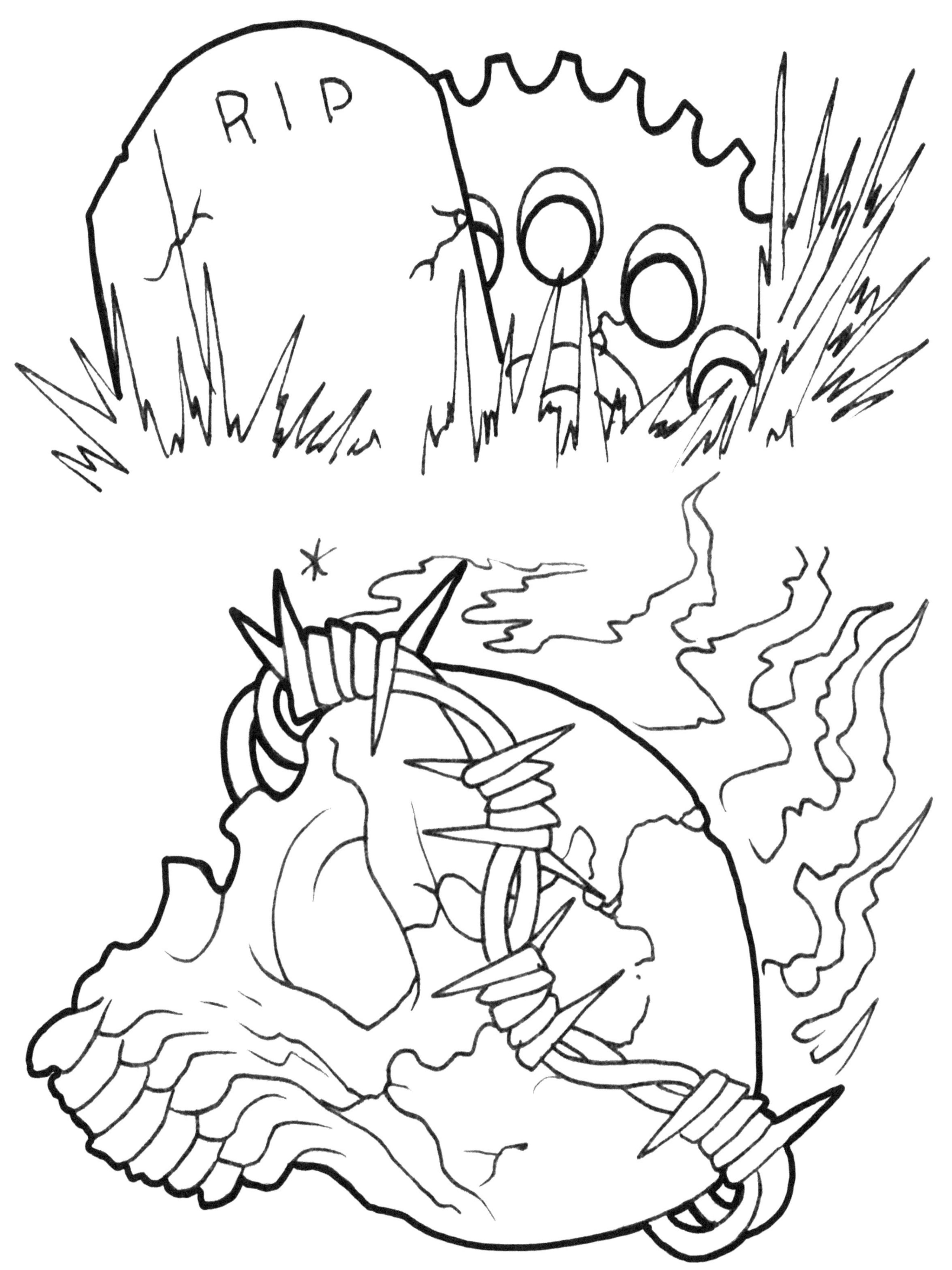
RIP

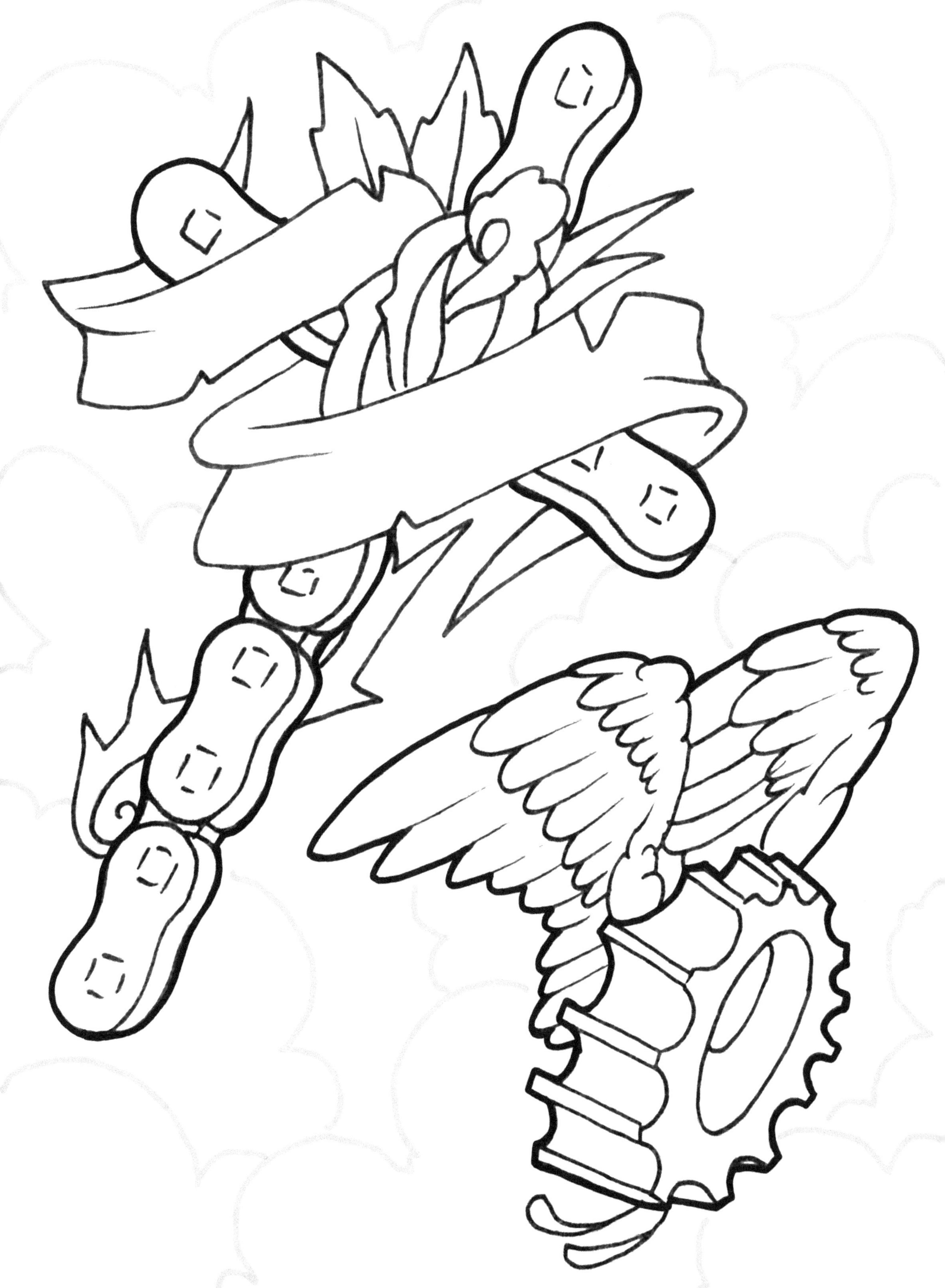

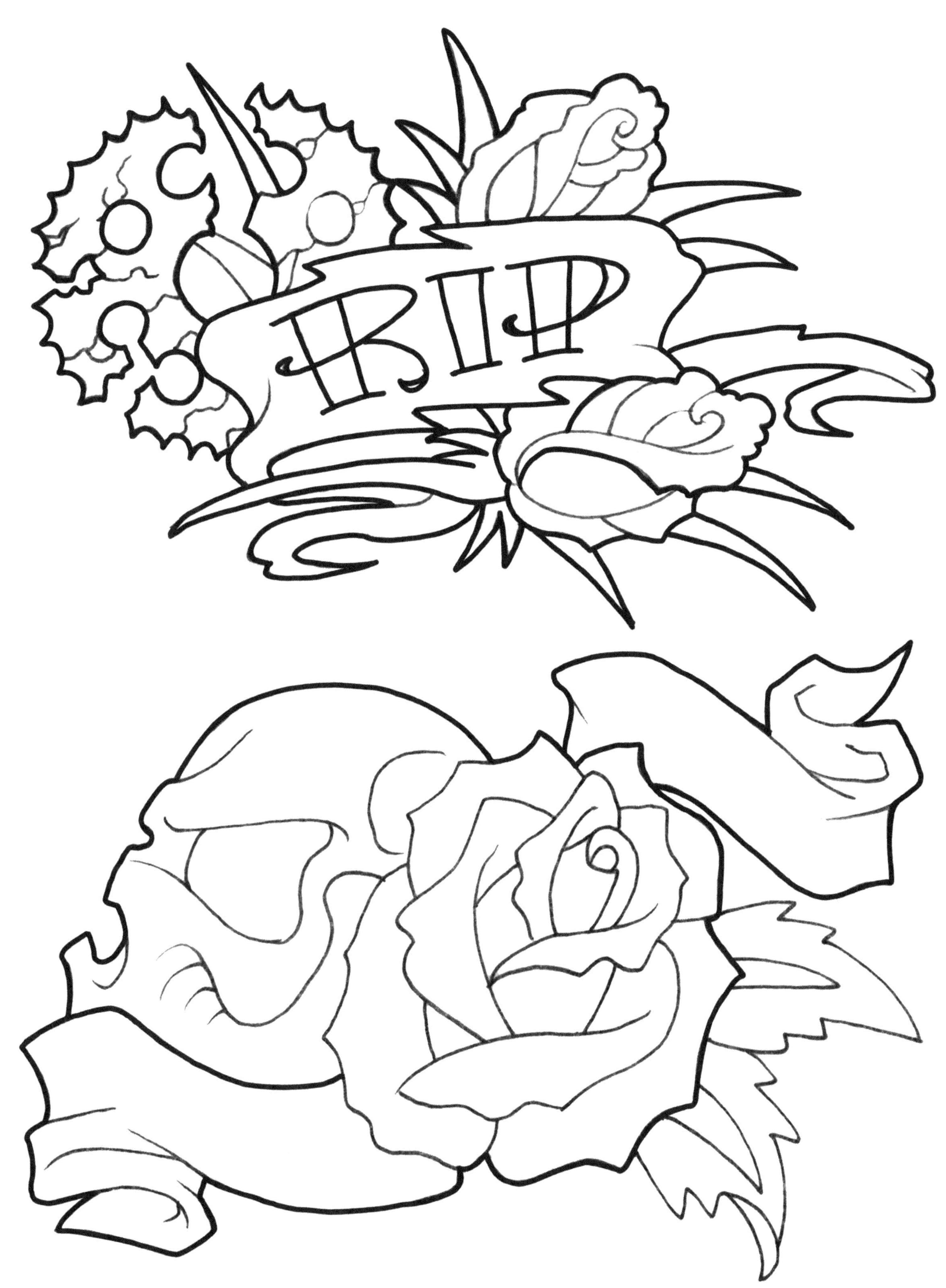
RIP

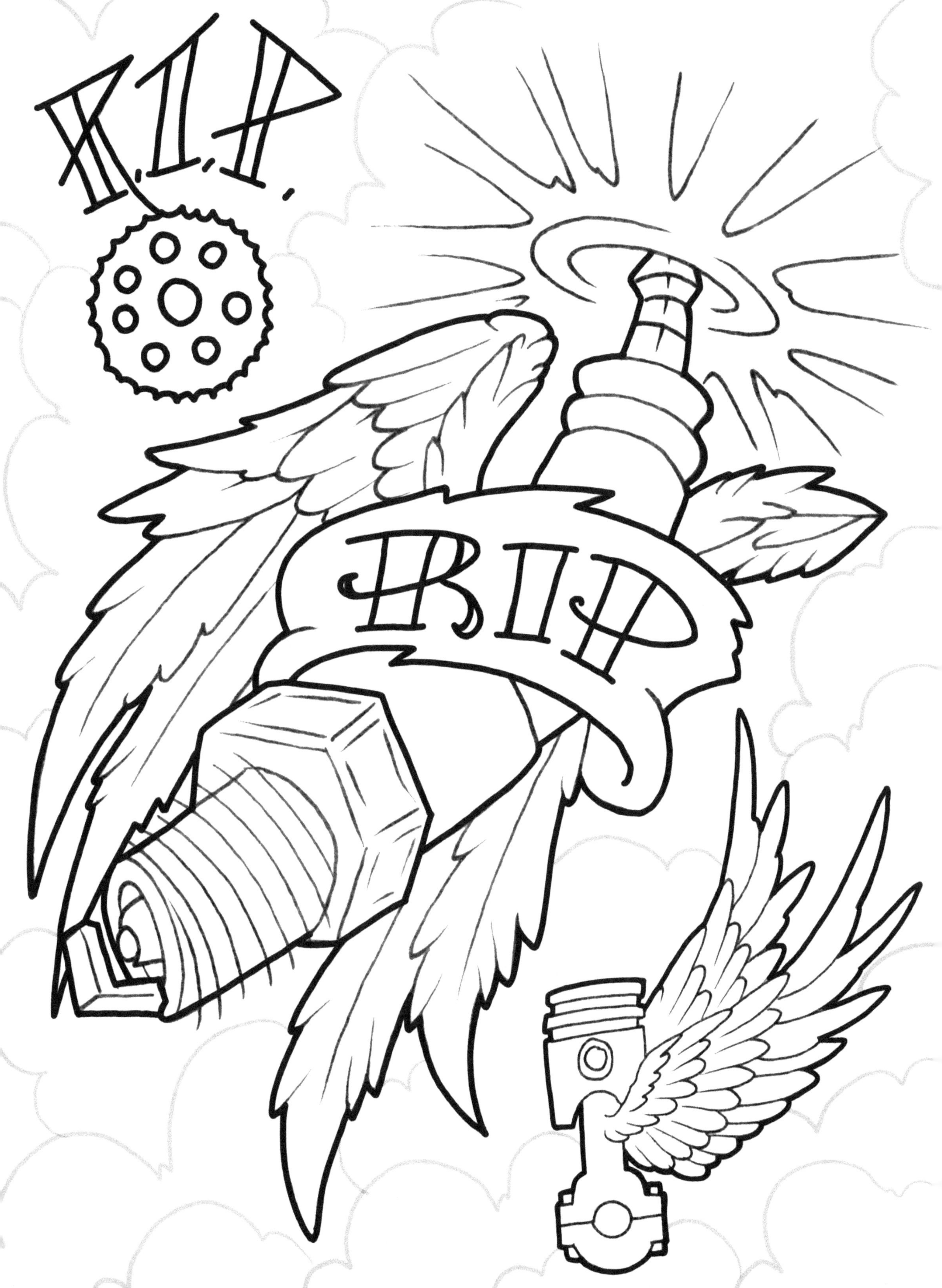
R.I.P.
RIP

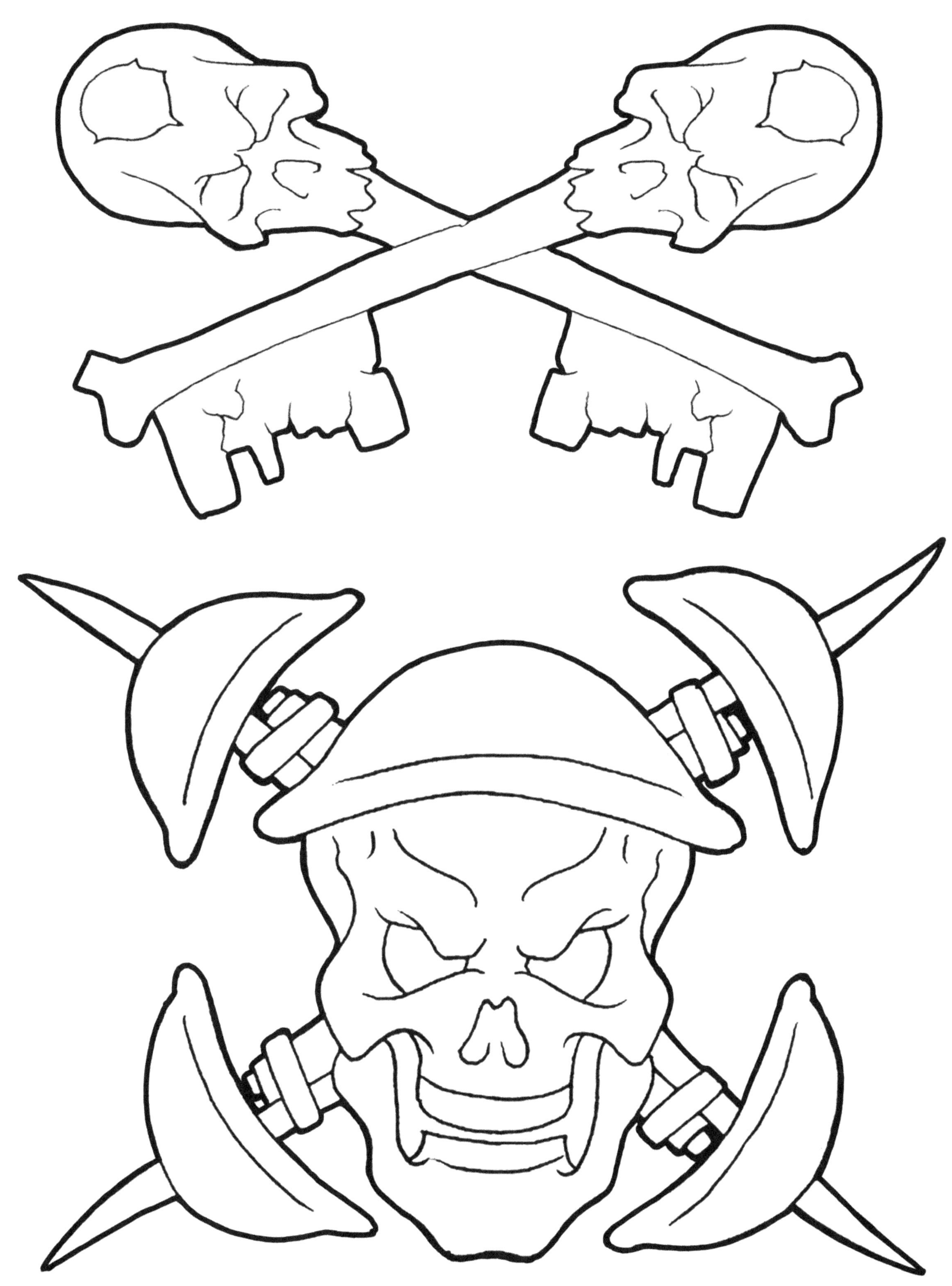

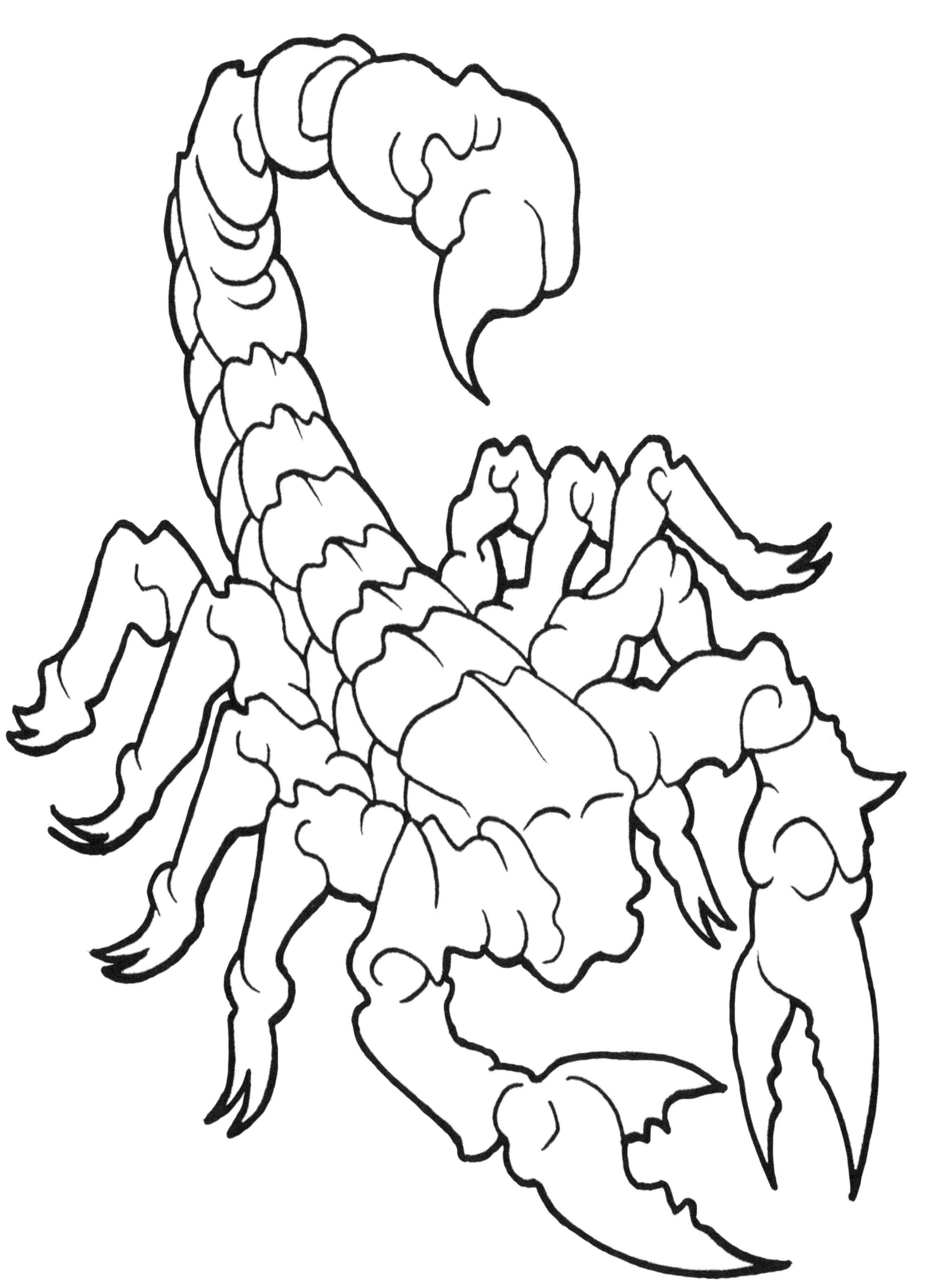

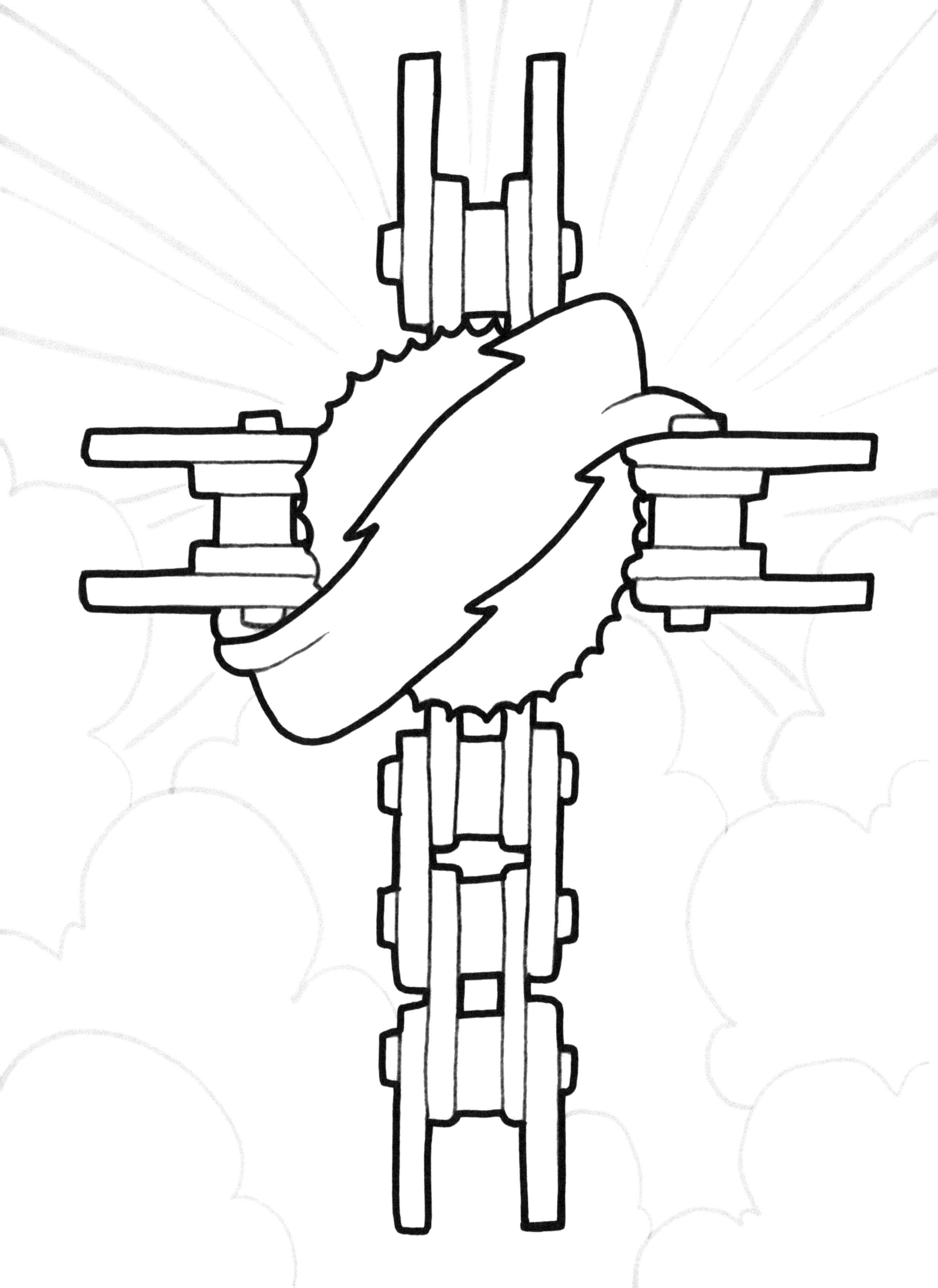

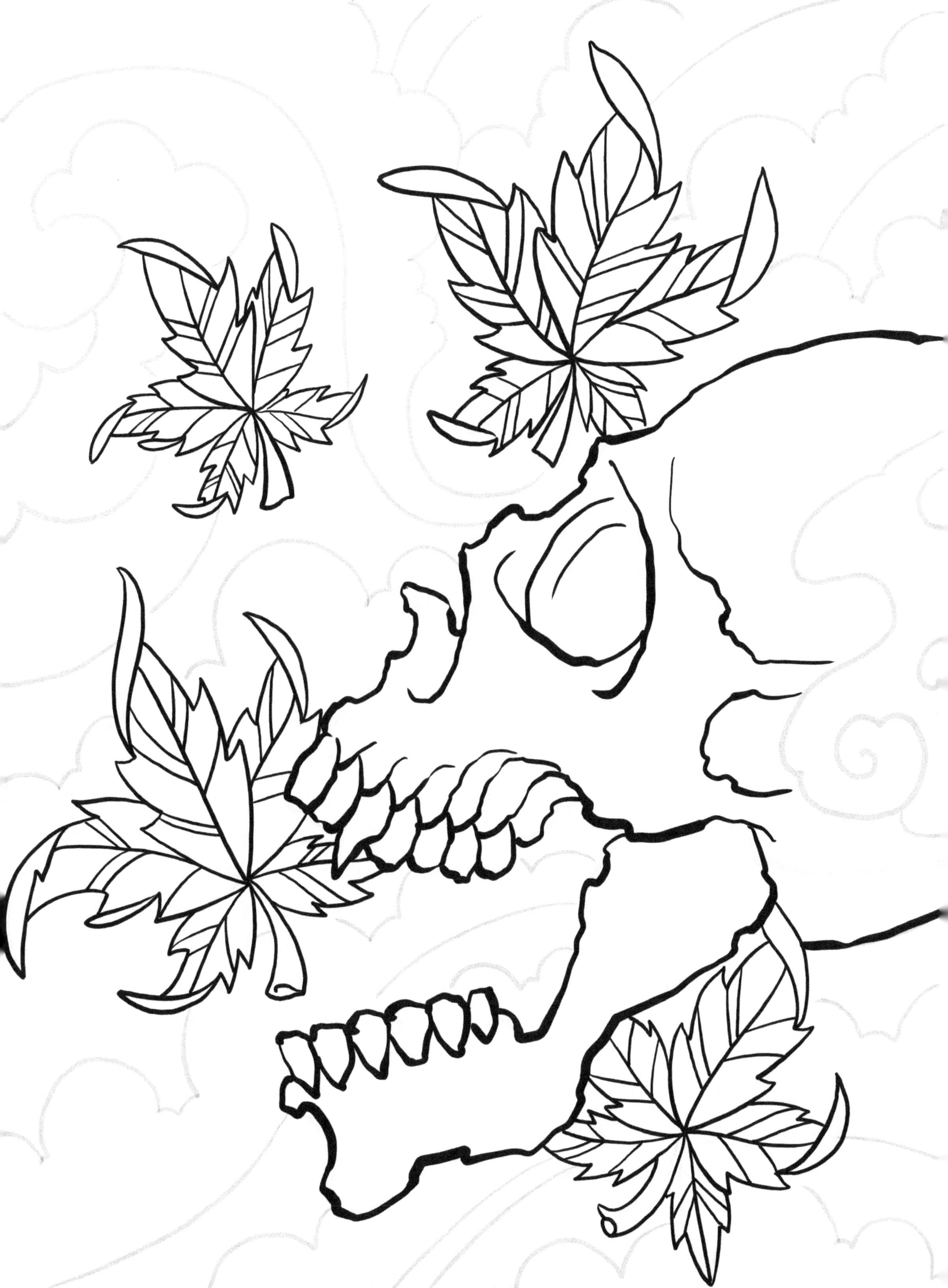

www.ingramcontent.com/pod-product-compliance
Lightning Source LLC
LaVergne TN
LVHW080926110826
845155LV00039B/218

* 9 7 8 1 9 4 8 1 8 7 3 1 2 *